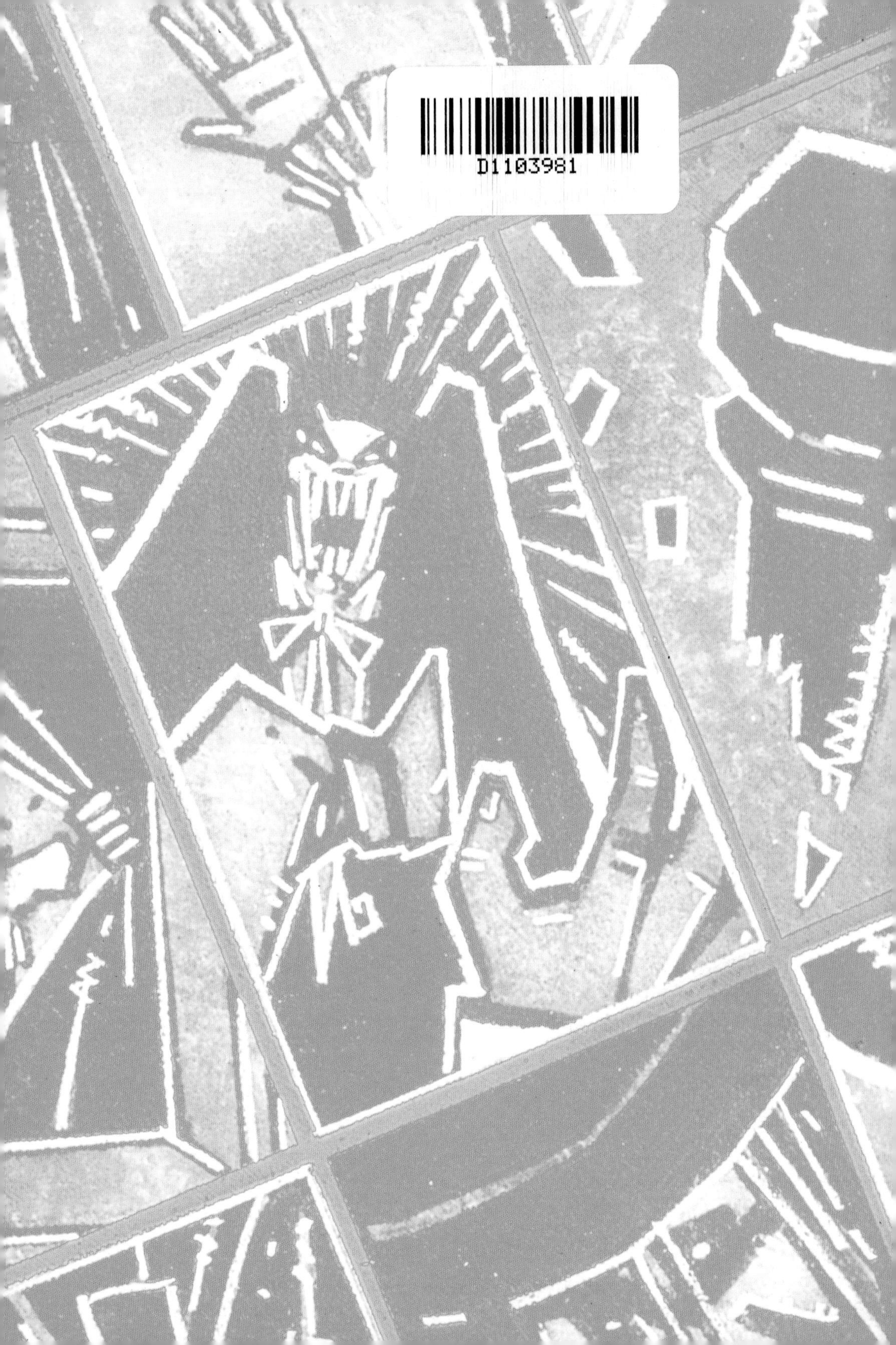

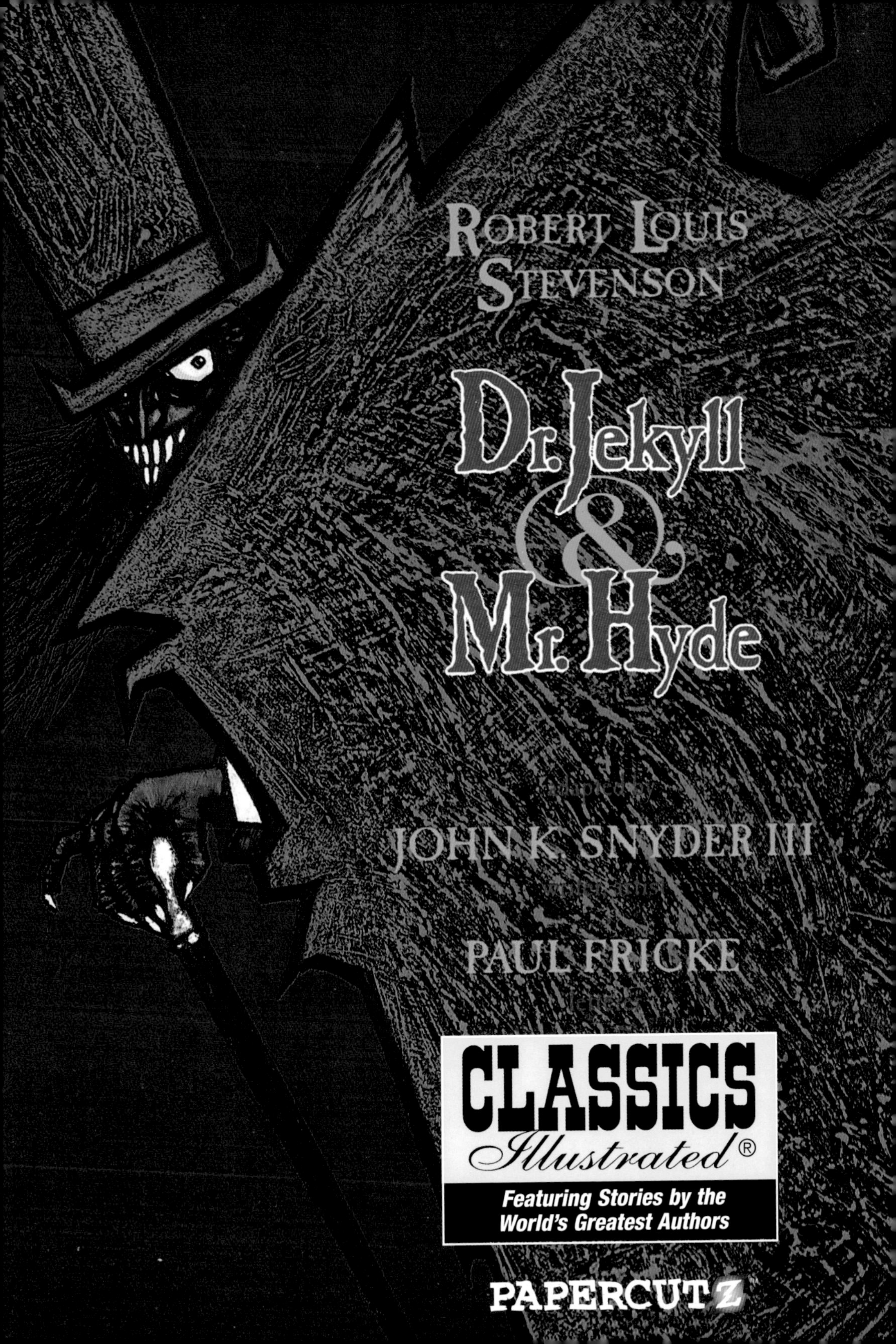
ROBERT LOUIS STEVENSON
Dr. Jekyll & Mr. Hyde
JOHN K. SNYDER III
PAUL FRICKE
CLASSICS Illustrated®
Featuring Stories by the World's Greatest Authors
PAPERCUTZ

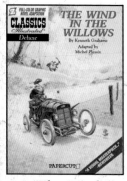

CLASSICS Illustrated ®

Featuring Stories by the World's Greatest Authors

#7

Dr. Jekyll & Mr. Hyde

By Robert Louis Stevenson
Adapted by John K. Snyder III

PAPERCUTZ™
New York

Robert Louis Stevenson's **Dr. Jekyll & Mr. Hyde** was born of a nightmare, from which his wife, Fanny – alerted by her husband's screams – roused him. "Why did you wake me?" Stevenson asked. "I was dreaming a fine bogey tale." Published in 1886, three years after the release of the highly popular Treasure Island, the novel was a tremendous success; some 40,000 copies were sold in six months which made **Dr. Jekyll & Mr. Hyde** one of the best-selling books of its time.

Although piqued by Stevenson's refusal to take his art seriously ("Fiction is to grown men what play is to the child," he once commented), critics have grudgingly praised his perceptive insight into the complex mixture of good and evil that constitutes the personality. Jekyll is not all good, and Hyde is not all evil. Rather, in Jekyll, there already exists a dark side, and, in Hyde, there remains a bit of good. The drug does not so much metamorphosize Jekyll, as it unleashes and empowers his hidden evil side. It is Stevenson's portrayal of that process, some scholars have suggested, that accounts for the novel's continued popularity: it gives a frightening yet fascinating voice to our own fears of uncaging our personal inner monsters.

Dr. Jekyll & Mr. Hyde
By Robert Louis Stevenson
Adapted by John K. Snyder III
Wade Roberts, Original Editorial Director
Alex Wald, Original Art Director
Production by Chris Nelson and Shelly Dutchak
Classics Illustrated Historians – John Haufe and William B. Jones Jr.
Editorial Assistant -- Michael Petranek
Jim Salicrup
Editor-in-Chief

ISBN: 978-1-59707-171-0

Printed in China
September 2009 by Regent Publishing
6/F, Hang Tung Resource Centre,
No. 18 A Kung Ngam Village Road,
Shau Kei Wan, Hong Kong

Distributed by Macmillan.
10 9 8 7 6 5 4 3 2 1

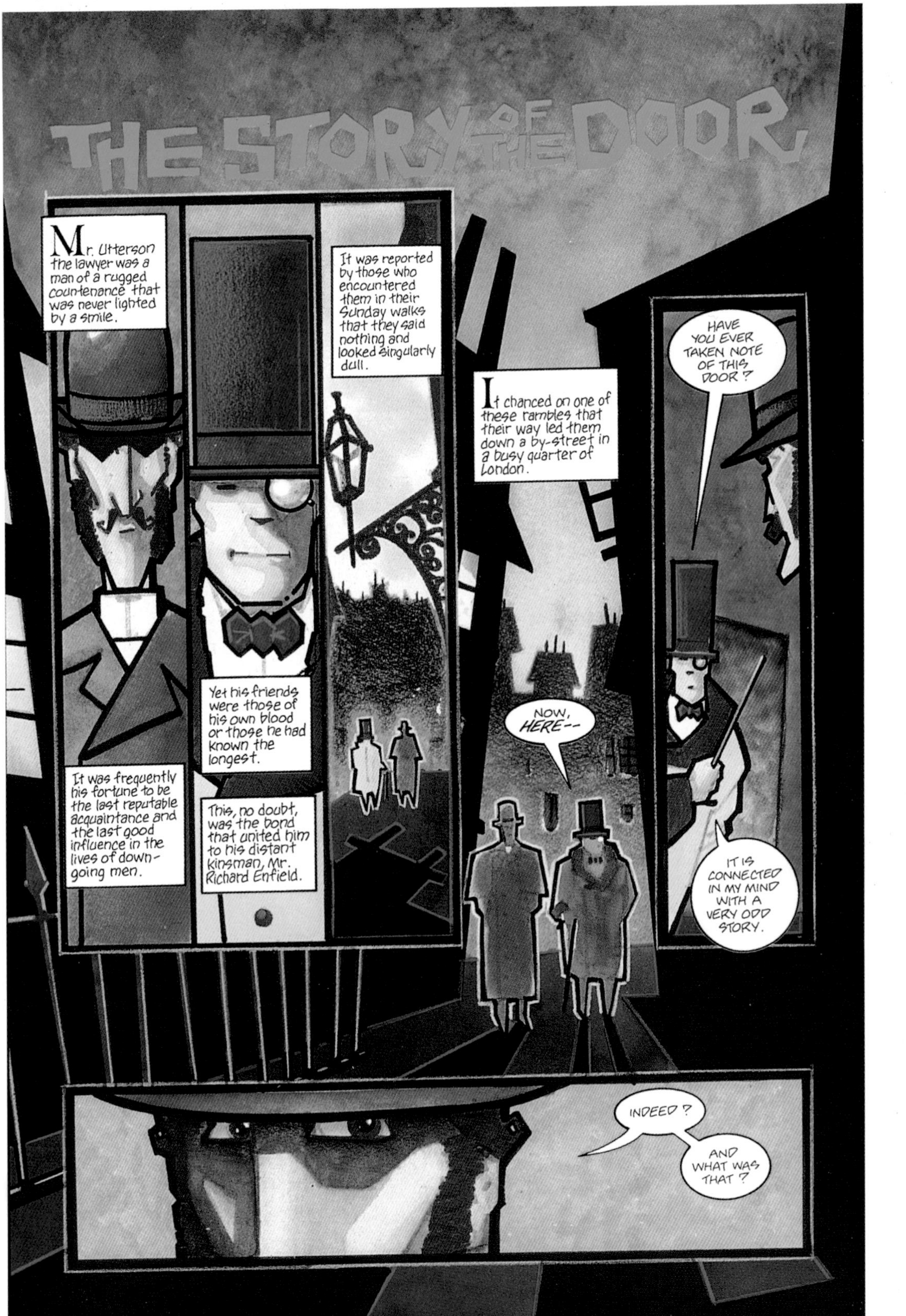
THE STORY OF THE DOOR
Mr. Utterson the lawyer was a man of a rugged countenance that was never lighted by a smile.
It was frequently his fortune to be the last reputable acquaintance and the last good influence in the lives of down-going men.
Yet his friends were those of his own blood or those he had known the longest.
This, no doubt, was the bond that united him to his distant kinsman, Mr. Richard Enfield.
It was reported by those who encountered them in their Sunday walks that they said nothing and looked singularly dull.
It chanced on one of these rambles that their way led them down a by-street in a busy quarter of London.
NOW, HERE--
HAVE YOU EVER TAKEN NOTE OF THIS DOOR ?
IT IS CONNECTED IN MY MIND WITH A VERY ODD STORY.
INDEED ?
AND WHAT WAS THAT ?

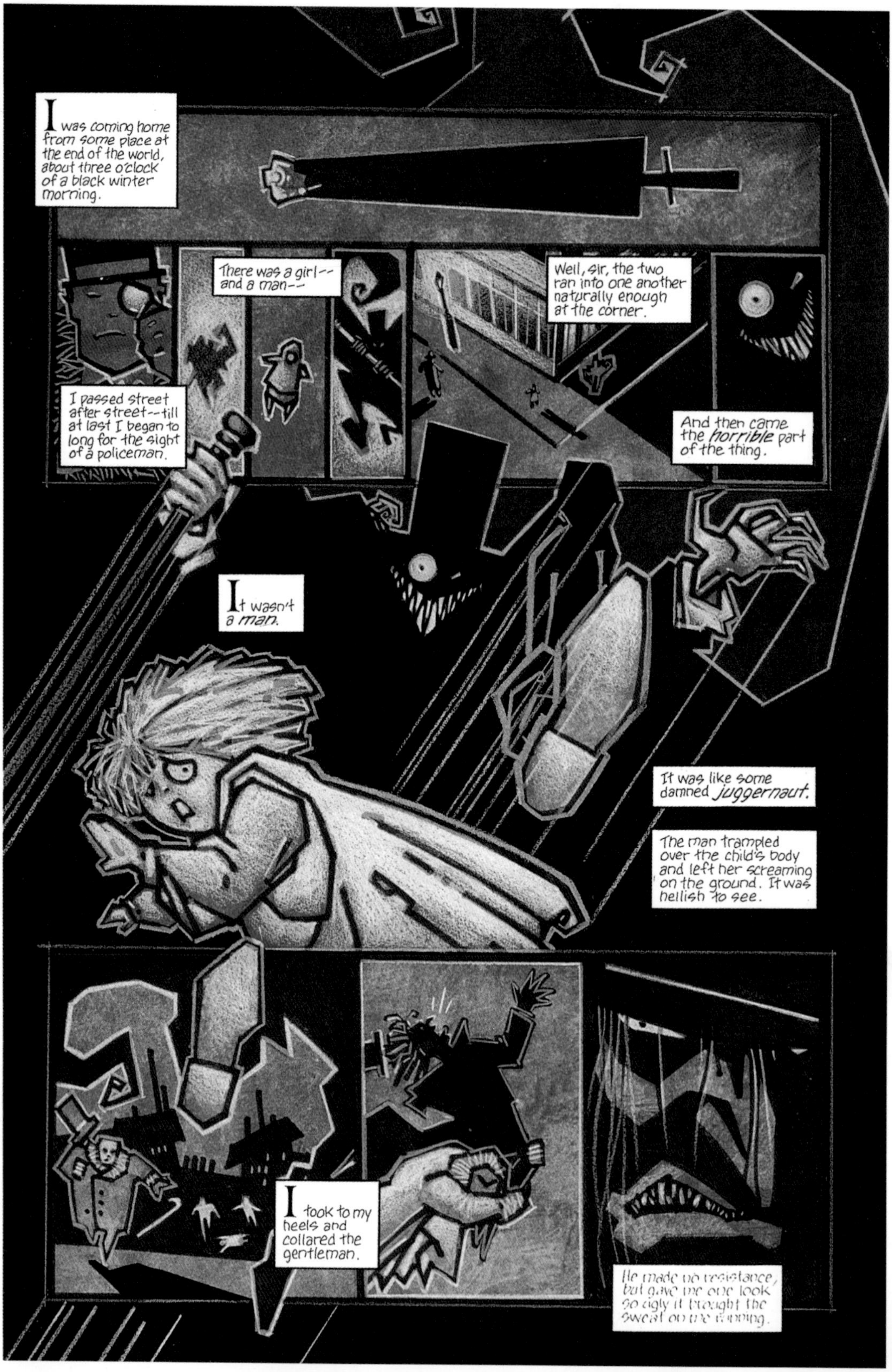
I was coming home from some place at the end of the world, about three o'clock of a black winter morning.
I passed street after street--till at last I began to long for the sight of a policeman.
There was a girl-- and a man--
Well, sir, the two ran into one another naturally enough at the corner.
And then came the *horrible* part of the thing.
It wasn't a *man*.
It was like some damned *juggernaut*.
The man trampled over the child's body and left her screaming on the ground. It was hellish to see.
I took to my heels and collared the gentleman.
He made no resistance, but gave me one look so ugly it brought the sweat on me running.

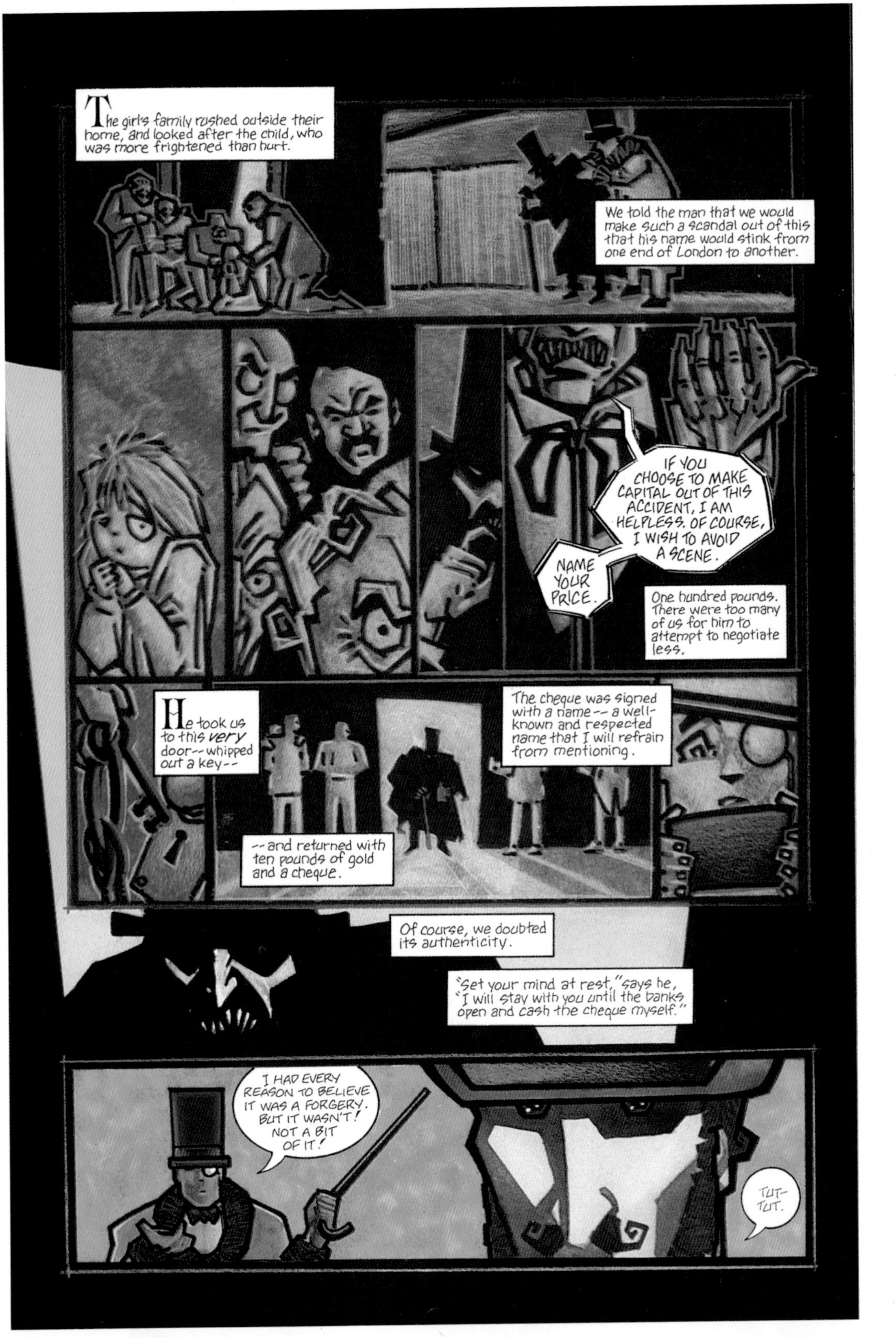
The girl's family rushed outside their home, and looked after the child, who was more frightened than hurt.
We told the man that we would make such a scandal out of this that his name would stink from one end of London to another.
IF YOU CHOOSE TO MAKE CAPITAL OUT OF THIS ACCIDENT, I AM HELPLESS. OF COURSE, I WISH TO AVOID A SCENE.
NAME YOUR PRICE.
One hundred pounds. There were too many of us for him to attempt to negotiate less.
He took us to this *very* door--whipped out a key--
--and returned with ten pounds of gold and a cheque.
The cheque was signed with a name--a well-known and respected name that I will refrain from mentioning.
Of course, we doubted its authenticity.
"Set your mind at rest," says he, "I will stay with you until the banks open and cash the cheque myself."
I HAD EVERY REASON TO BELIEVE IT WAS A FORGERY. BUT IT WASN'T! NOT A BIT OF IT!
TUT-TUT.

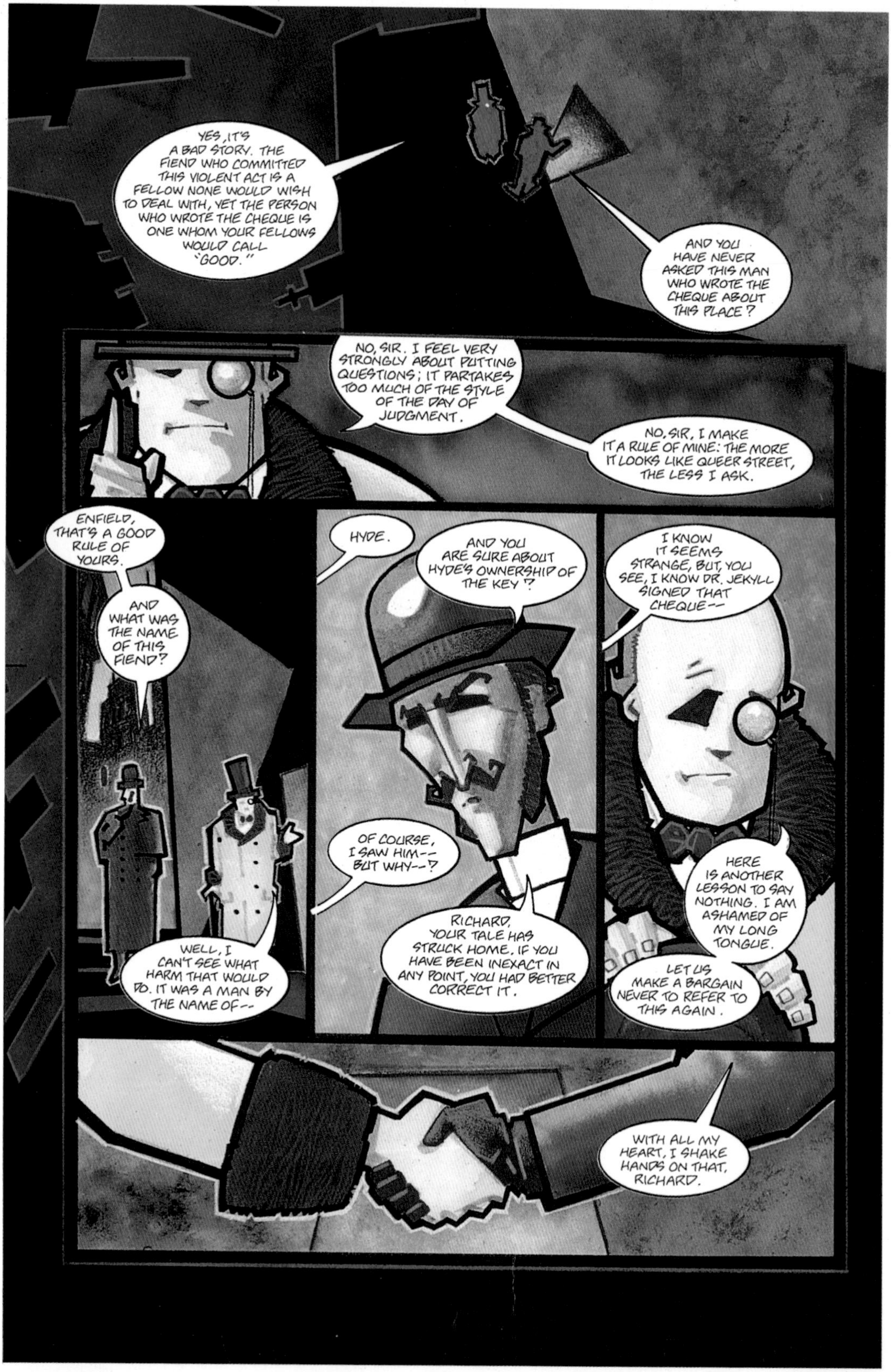
YES, IT'S A BAD STORY. THE FIEND WHO COMMITTED THIS VIOLENT ACT IS A FELLOW NONE WOULD WISH TO DEAL WITH, YET THE PERSON WHO WROTE THE CHEQUE IS ONE WHOM YOUR FELLOWS WOULD CALL "GOOD."
AND YOU HAVE NEVER ASKED THIS MAN WHO WROTE THE CHEQUE ABOUT THIS PLACE?
NO, SIR. I FEEL VERY STRONGLY ABOUT PUTTING QUESTIONS; IT PARTAKES TOO MUCH OF THE STYLE OF THE DAY OF JUDGMENT.
NO, SIR, I MAKE IT A RULE OF MINE: THE MORE IT LOOKS LIKE QUEER STREET, THE LESS I ASK.
ENFIELD, THAT'S A GOOD RULE OF YOURS.
AND WHAT WAS THE NAME OF THIS FIEND?
WELL, I CAN'T SEE WHAT HARM THAT WOULD DO. IT WAS A MAN BY THE NAME OF--
HYDE.
AND YOU ARE SURE ABOUT HYDE'S OWNERSHIP OF THE KEY?
OF COURSE, I SAW HIM-- BUT WHY--?
RICHARD, YOUR TALE HAS STRUCK HOME. IF YOU HAVE BEEN INEXACT IN ANY POINT, YOU HAD BETTER CORRECT IT.
I KNOW IT SEEMS STRANGE, BUT, YOU SEE, I KNOW DR. JEKYLL SIGNED THAT CHEQUE--
HERE IS ANOTHER LESSON TO SAY NOTHING. I AM ASHAMED OF MY LONG TONGUE.
LET US MAKE A BARGAIN NEVER TO REFER TO THIS AGAIN.
WITH ALL MY HEART, I SHAKE HANDS ON THAT, RICHARD.

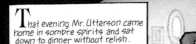

That evening Mr. Utterson came home in sombre spirits and sat down to dinner without relish.

As soon as the tablecloth was taken away, he took up a candle and went into his business room.

There he opened his safe, took from the most private part of it a document endorsed on the envelope as Dr. Jekyll's will, and sat down with a clouded brow to study its contents.

Utterson wanted nothing to do with Jekyll's will, and had refused to lend the least assistance in the making of it.

It stated that, in the case of the decease or disappearance of more than three months of Henry Jekyll M.D., all of his possessions were to pass into the hands of his "friend and benefactor Edward Hyde."

This document had long been the lawyer's eyesore.

It was already bad enough when Hyde was but a name of which he could learn nothing.

It was worse when it began to be clothed upon with detestable attributes. And out of the shifting mists that had baffled him so, leapt the sudden presence of a fiend.

I THOUGHT IT WAS MADNESS--

AND NOW I FEAR IT IS DISGRACE.

IF ANYONE KNOWS OF THIS STRANGE ALLIANCE, IT WILL BE LANYON.

I SUPPOSE, LANYON, YOU AND I MUST BE THE TWO OLDEST FRIENDS THAT HENRY JEKYLL HAS?

I WISH THE FRIENDS WERE YOUNGER, BUT I SUPPOSE WE ARE. AND WHAT OF THAT? I SEE LITTLE OF HIM NOW.

INDEED? I THOUGHT YOU HAD A COMMON INTEREST.

WE HAD--BUT IT HAS BEEN MORE THAN TEN YEARS SINCE HENRY JEKYLL BECAME TOO FANCIFUL FOR ME.

This little spirit of temper was a relief to Utterson.

SUCH UNSCIENTIFIC BALDERDASH.

HE BEGAN TO GO WRONG-- WRONG IN MIND.

"They have only differed on some point of science," he thought; "It is nothing worse than that!"

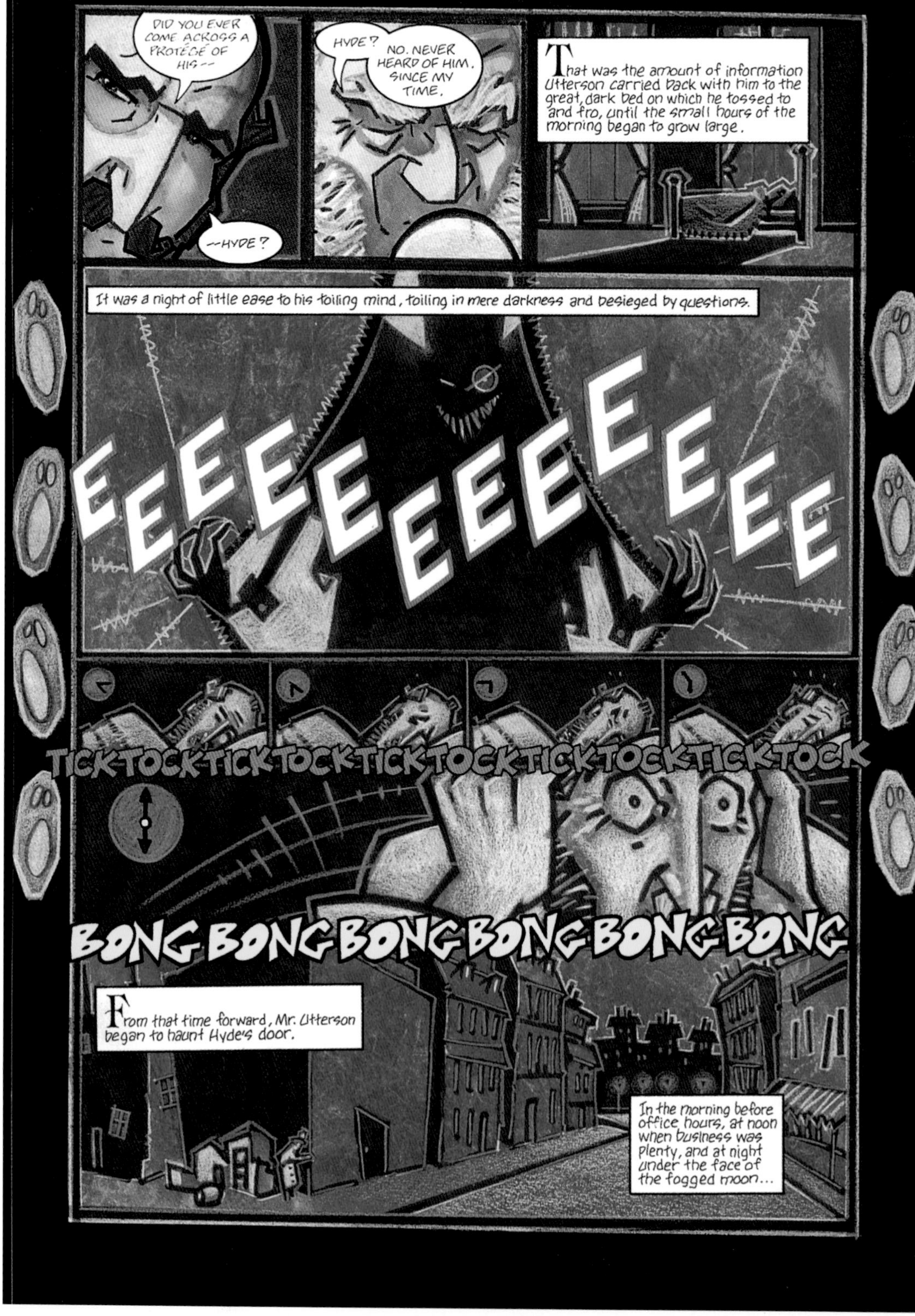
DID YOU EVER COME ACROSS A PROTÉGÉ OF HIS --
--HYDE?
HYDE?
NO. NEVER HEARD OF HIM. SINCE MY TIME.
That was the amount of information Utterson carried back with him to the great, dark bed on which he tossed to and fro, until the small hours of the morning began to grow large.
It was a night of little ease to his toiling mind, toiling in mere darkness and besieged by questions.
EEEEEEEEEEEE
TICK TOCK TICK TOCK TICK TOCK TICK TOCK TICK TOCK
BONG BONG BONG BONG BONG BONG
From that time forward, Mr. Utterson began to haunt Hyde's door.
In the morning before office hours, at noon when business was plenty, and at night under the face of the fogged moon...

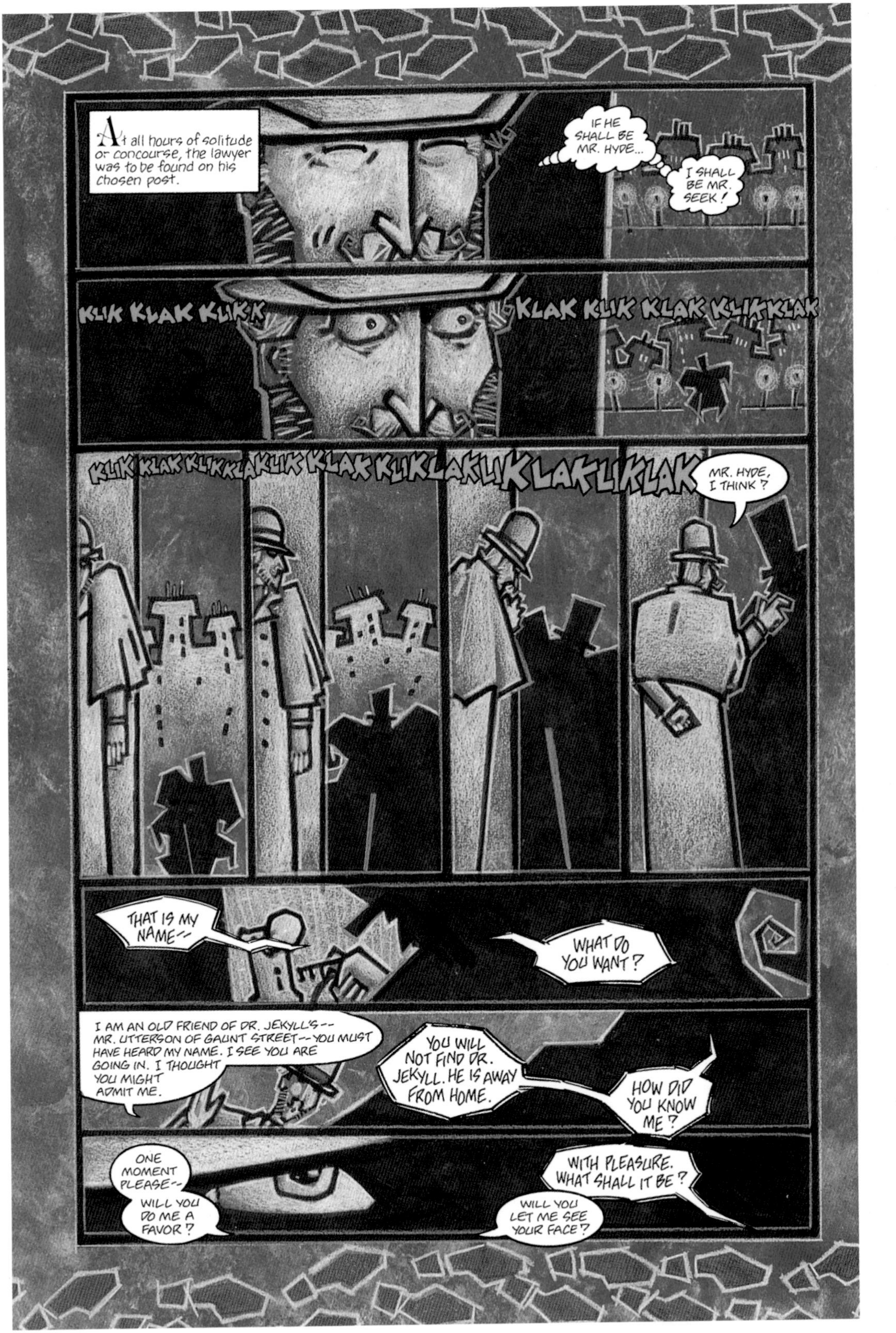
At all hours of solitude or concourse, the lawyer was to be found on his chosen post.
IF HE SHALL BE MR. HYDE...
I SHALL BE MR. SEEK!
KLIK KLAK KLIK K
KLAK KLIK KLAK KLIKKLAK
KLIK KLAK KLIKKLAKLIK KLAK KLIKLAKLIKLAKLIKLAK
MR. HYDE, I THINK?
THAT IS MY NAME--
WHAT DO YOU WANT?
I AM AN OLD FRIEND OF DR. JEKYLL'S-- MR. UTTERSON OF GAUNT STREET--YOU MUST HAVE HEARD MY NAME. I SEE YOU ARE GOING IN. I THOUGHT YOU MIGHT ADMIT ME.
YOU WILL NOT FIND DR. JEKYLL. HE IS AWAY FROM HOME.
HOW DID YOU KNOW ME?
ONE MOMENT PLEASE--
WILL YOU DO ME A FAVOR?
WITH PLEASURE. WHAT SHALL IT BE?
WILL YOU LET ME SEE YOUR FACE?

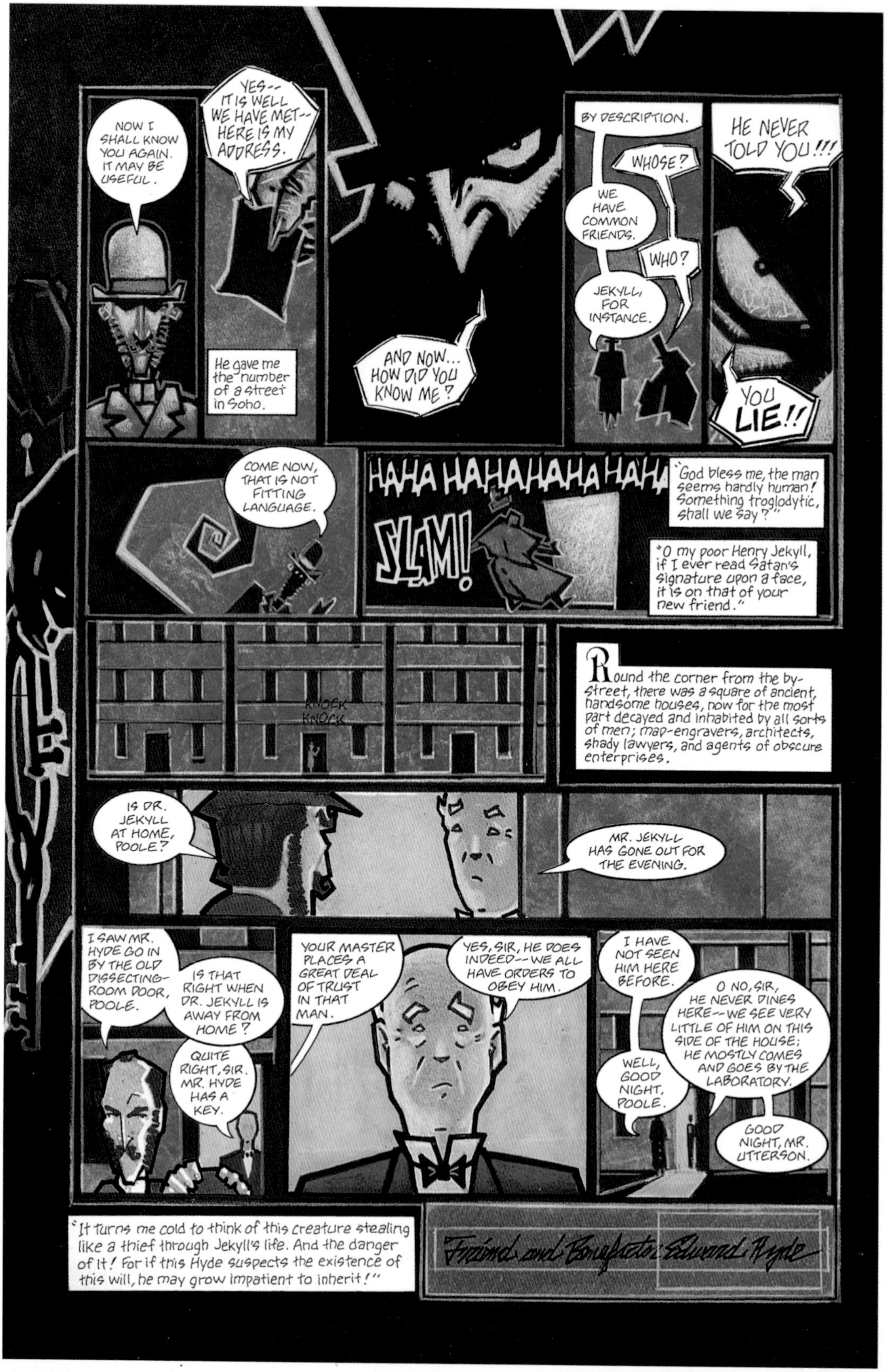
NOW I SHALL KNOW YOU AGAIN. IT MAY BE USEFUL.
YES-- IT IS WELL WE HAVE MET-- HERE IS MY ADDRESS.
He gave me the number of a street in Soho.
AND NOW... HOW DID YOU KNOW ME?
BY DESCRIPTION.
WHOSE?
WE HAVE COMMON FRIENDS.
WHO?
JEKYLL, FOR INSTANCE.
HE NEVER TOLD YOU!!!
YOU LIE!!
COME NOW, THAT IS NOT FITTING LANGUAGE.
HAHA HAHAHAHA HAHA
SLAM!
"God bless me, the man seems hardly human! Something troglodytic, shall we say?"
"O my poor Henry Jekyll, if I ever read Satan's signature upon a face, it is on that of your new friend."
Round the corner from the by-street, there was a square of ancient, handsome houses, now for the most part decayed and inhabited by all sorts of men; map-engravers, architects, shady lawyers, and agents of obscure enterprises.
KNOCK KNOCK
IS DR. JEKYLL AT HOME, POOLE?
MR. JEKYLL HAS GONE OUT FOR THE EVENING.
I SAW MR. HYDE GO IN BY THE OLD DISSECTING-ROOM DOOR, POOLE.
IS THAT RIGHT WHEN DR. JEKYLL IS AWAY FROM HOME?
QUITE RIGHT, SIR. MR. HYDE HAS A KEY.
YOUR MASTER PLACES A GREAT DEAL OF TRUST IN THAT MAN.
YES, SIR, HE DOES INDEED-- WE ALL HAVE ORDERS TO OBEY HIM.
I HAVE NOT SEEN HIM HERE BEFORE.
O NO, SIR, HE NEVER DINES HERE-- WE SEE VERY LITTLE OF HIM ON THIS SIDE OF THE HOUSE; HE MOSTLY COMES AND GOES BY THE LABORATORY.
WELL, GOOD NIGHT, POOLE.
GOOD NIGHT, MR. UTTERSON.
"It turns me cold to think of this creature stealing like a thief through Jekyll's life. And the danger of it! For if this Hyde suspects the existence of this will, he may grow impatient to inherit!"
Friend and Benefactor Edward Hyde

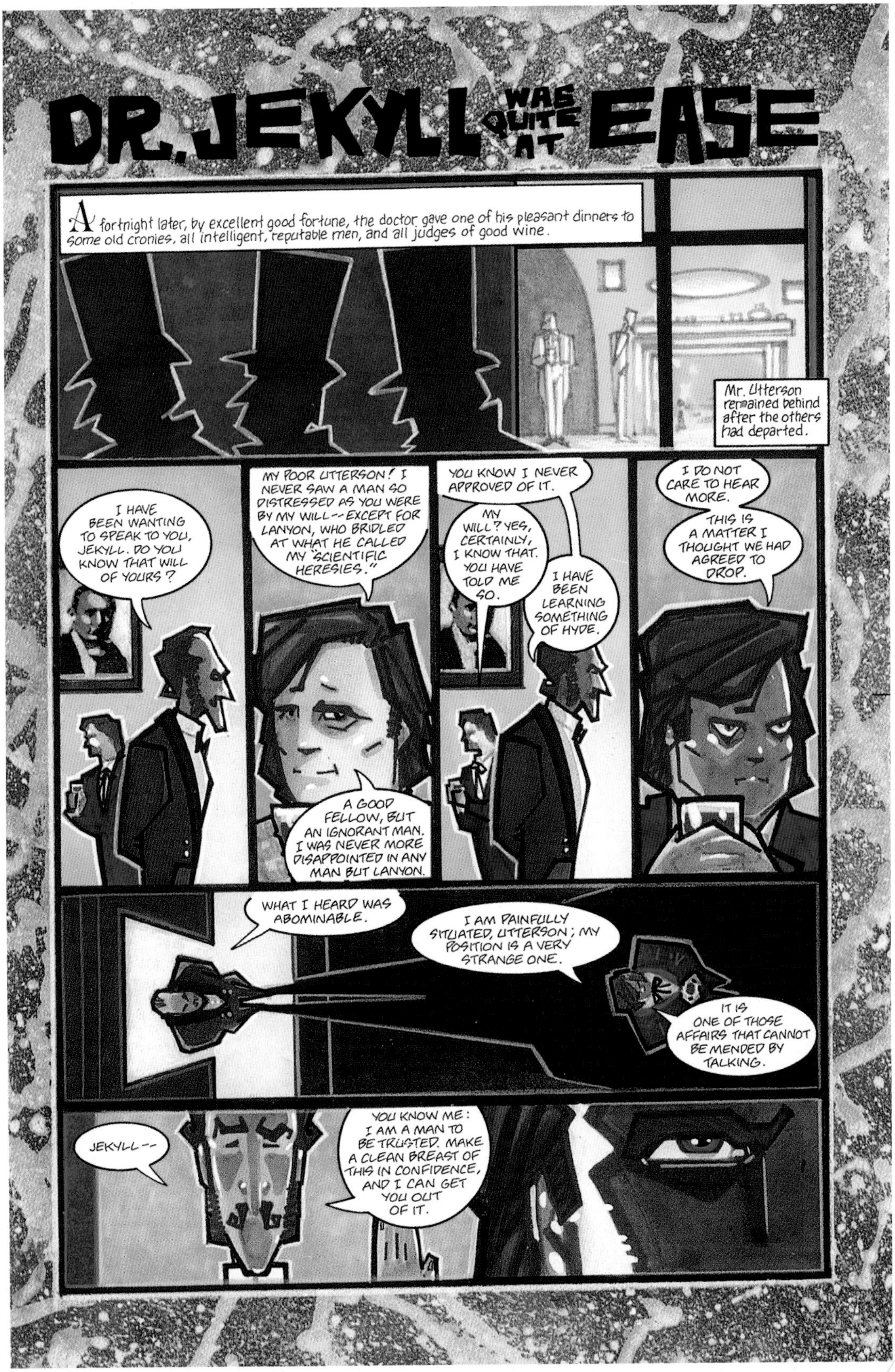
DR. JEKYLL WAS QUITE AT EASE
A fortnight later, by excellent good fortune, the doctor gave one of his pleasant dinners to some old cronies, all intelligent, reputable men, and all judges of good wine.
Mr. Utterson remained behind after the others had departed.
I HAVE BEEN WANTING TO SPEAK TO YOU, JEKYLL. DO YOU KNOW THAT WILL OF YOURS?
MY POOR UTTERSON! I NEVER SAW A MAN SO DISTRESSED AS YOU WERE BY MY WILL--EXCEPT FOR LANYON, WHO BRIDLED AT WHAT HE CALLED MY "SCIENTIFIC HERESIES."
A GOOD FELLOW, BUT AN IGNORANT MAN. I WAS NEVER MORE DISAPPOINTED IN ANY MAN BUT LANYON.
YOU KNOW I NEVER APPROVED OF IT.
MY WILL? YES, CERTAINLY, I KNOW THAT. YOU HAVE TOLD ME SO.
I HAVE BEEN LEARNING SOMETHING OF HYDE.
I DO NOT CARE TO HEAR MORE.
THIS IS A MATTER I THOUGHT WE HAD AGREED TO DROP.
WHAT I HEARD WAS ABOMINABLE.
I AM PAINFULLY SITUATED, UTTERSON; MY POSITION IS A VERY STRANGE ONE.
IT IS ONE OF THOSE AFFAIRS THAT CANNOT BE MENDED BY TALKING.
JEKYLL--
YOU KNOW ME: I AM A MAN TO BE TRUSTED. MAKE A CLEAN BREAST OF THIS IN CONFIDENCE, AND I CAN GET YOU OUT OF IT.

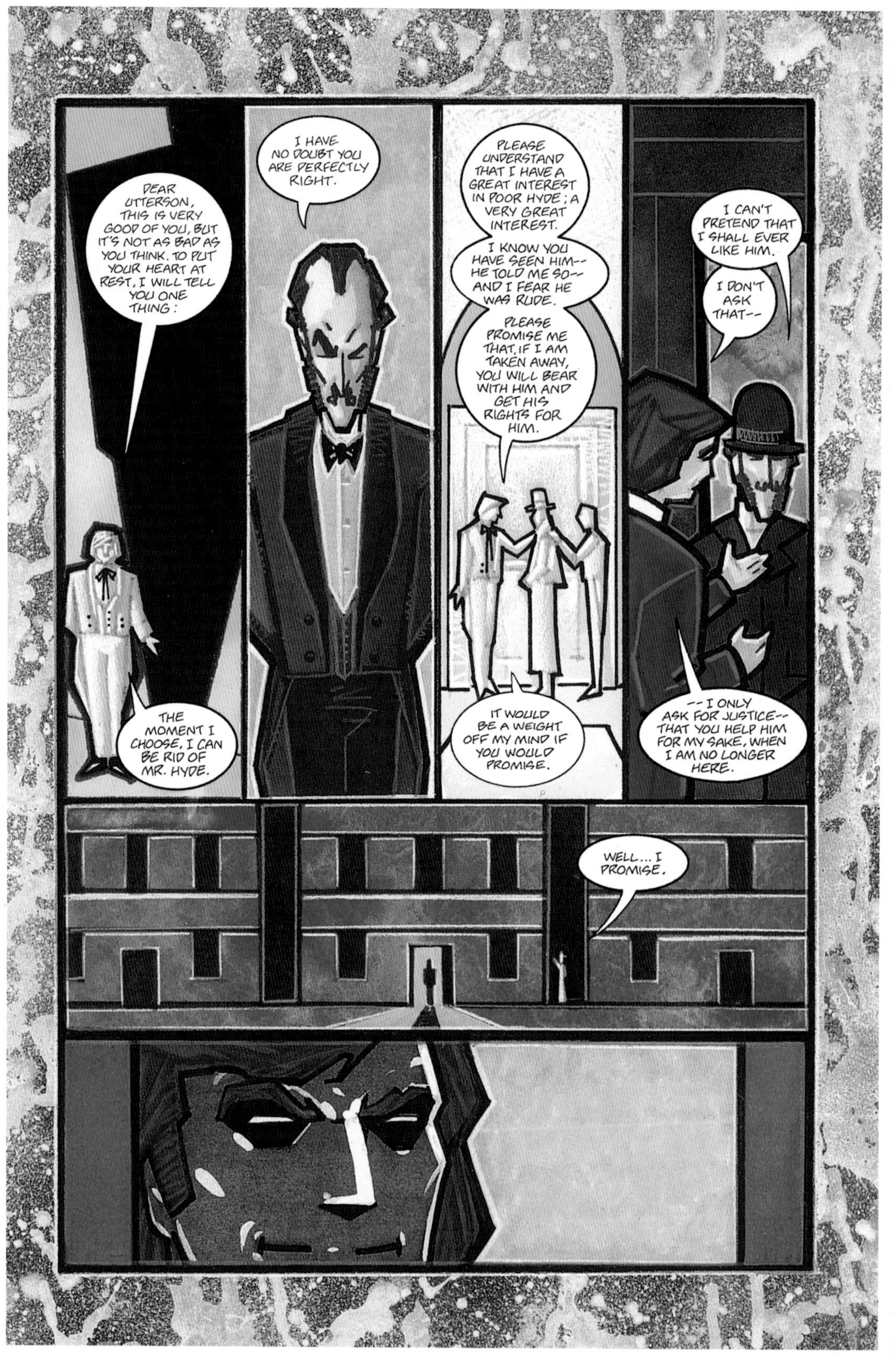
DEAR UTTERSON, THIS IS VERY GOOD OF YOU, BUT IT'S NOT AS BAD AS YOU THINK. TO PUT YOUR HEART AT REST, I WILL TELL YOU ONE THING:
THE MOMENT I CHOOSE, I CAN BE RID OF MR. HYDE.
I HAVE NO DOUBT YOU ARE PERFECTLY RIGHT.
PLEASE UNDERSTAND THAT I HAVE A GREAT INTEREST IN POOR HYDE; A VERY GREAT INTEREST.
I KNOW YOU HAVE SEEN HIM-- HE TOLD ME SO-- AND I FEAR HE WAS RUDE.
PLEASE PROMISE ME THAT, IF I AM TAKEN AWAY, YOU WILL BEAR WITH HIM AND GET HIS RIGHTS FOR HIM.
IT WOULD BE A WEIGHT OFF MY MIND IF YOU WOULD PROMISE.
I CAN'T PRETEND THAT I SHALL EVER LIKE HIM.
I DON'T ASK THAT--
--I ONLY ASK FOR JUSTICE-- THAT YOU HELP HIM FOR MY SAKE, WHEN I AM NO LONGER HERE.
WELL... I PROMISE.

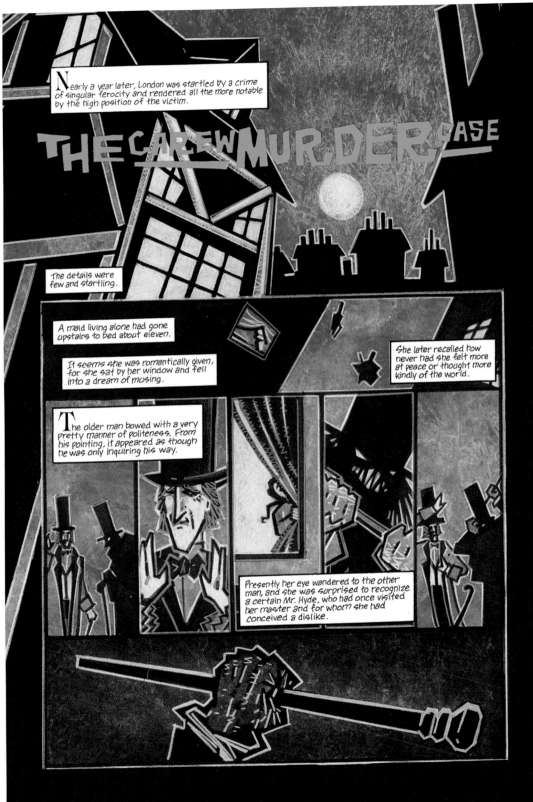

Nearly a year later, London was startled by a crime of singular ferocity and rendered all the more notable by the high position of the victim.

THE CAREW MURDER CASE

The details were few and startling.

A maid living alone had gone upstairs to bed about eleven.

It seems she was romantically given, for she sat by her window and fell into a dream of musing.

She later recalled how never had she felt more at peace or thought more kindly of the world.

The older man bowed with a very pretty manner of politeness. From his pointing, it appeared as though he was only inquiring his way.

Presently her eye wandered to the other man, and she was surprised to recognize a certain Mr. Hyde, who had once visited her master and for whom she had conceived a dislike.

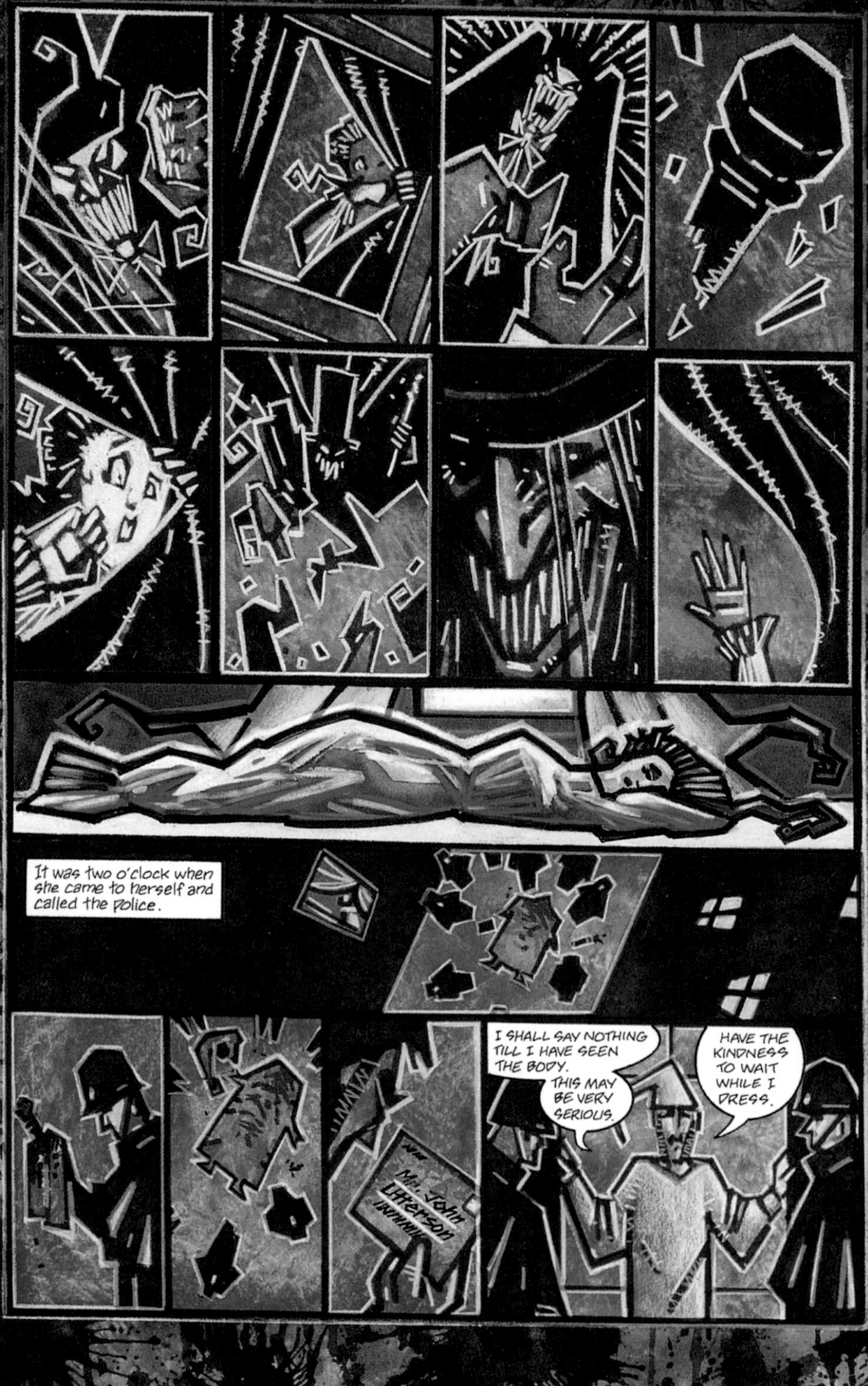
It was two o'clock when she came to herself and called the police.
Mr. John Utterson
I SHALL SAY NOTHING TILL I HAVE SEEN THE BODY.
THIS MAY BE VERY SERIOUS.
HAVE THE KINDNESS TO WAIT WHILE I DRESS.

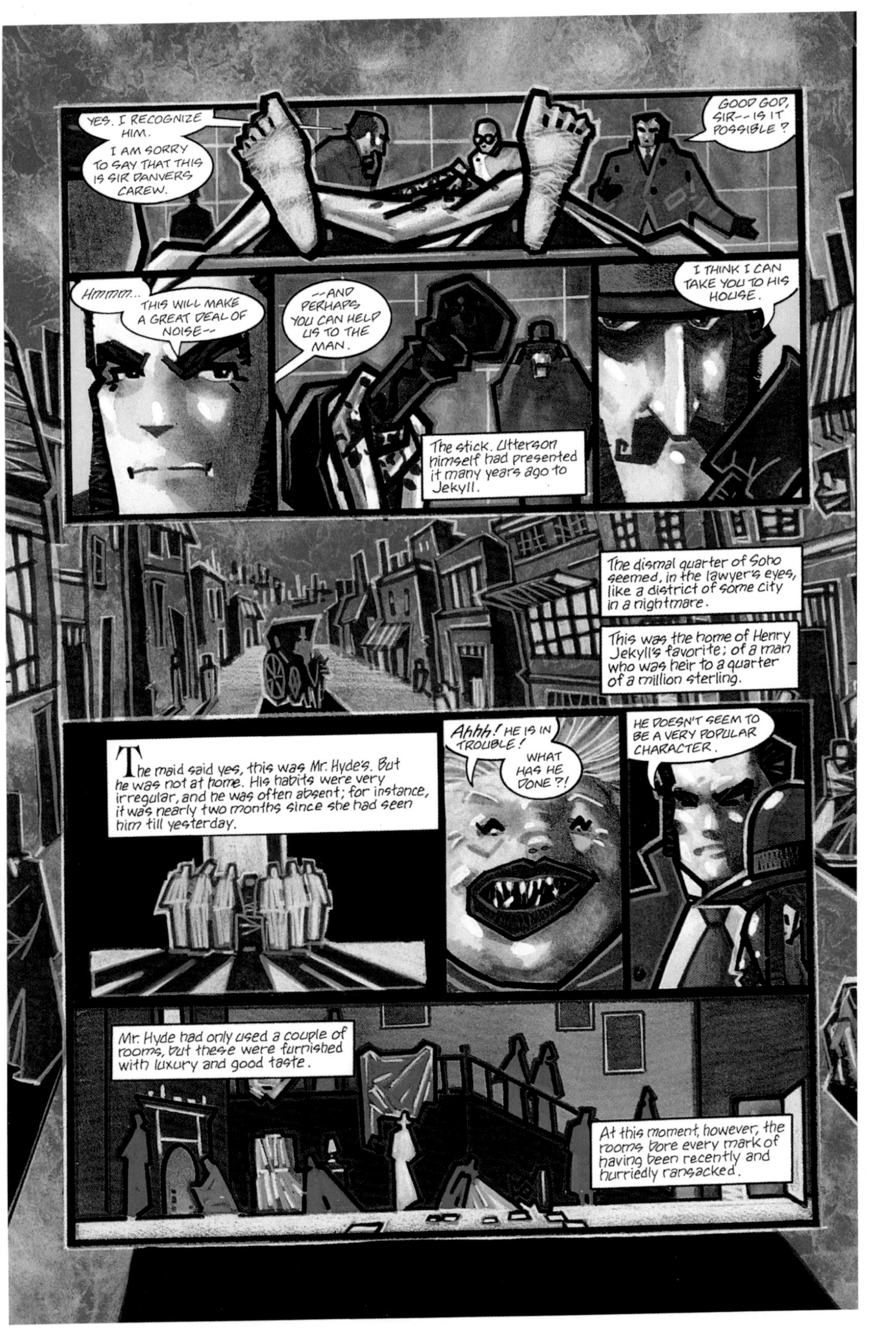
YES. I RECOGNIZE HIM. I AM SORRY TO SAY THAT THIS IS SIR DANVERS CAREW.
GOOD GOD, SIR-- IS IT POSSIBLE?
Hmmm... THIS WILL MAKE A GREAT DEAL OF NOISE--
--AND PERHAPS YOU CAN HELP US TO THE MAN.
The stick. Utterson himself had presented it many years ago to Jekyll.
I THINK I CAN TAKE YOU TO HIS HOUSE.
The dismal quarter of Soho seemed, in the lawyer's eyes, like a district of some city in a nightmare.
This was the home of Henry Jekyll's favorite; of a man who was heir to a quarter of a million sterling.
The maid said yes, this was Mr. Hyde's. But he was not at home. His habits were very irregular, and he was often absent; for instance, it was nearly two months since she had seen him till yesterday.
Ahhh! HE IS IN TROUBLE!
WHAT HAS HE DONE?!
HE DOESN'T SEEM TO BE A VERY POPULAR CHARACTER.
Mr. Hyde had only used a couple of rooms, but these were furnished with luxury and good taste.
At this moment, however, the rooms bore every mark of having been recently and hurriedly ransacked.

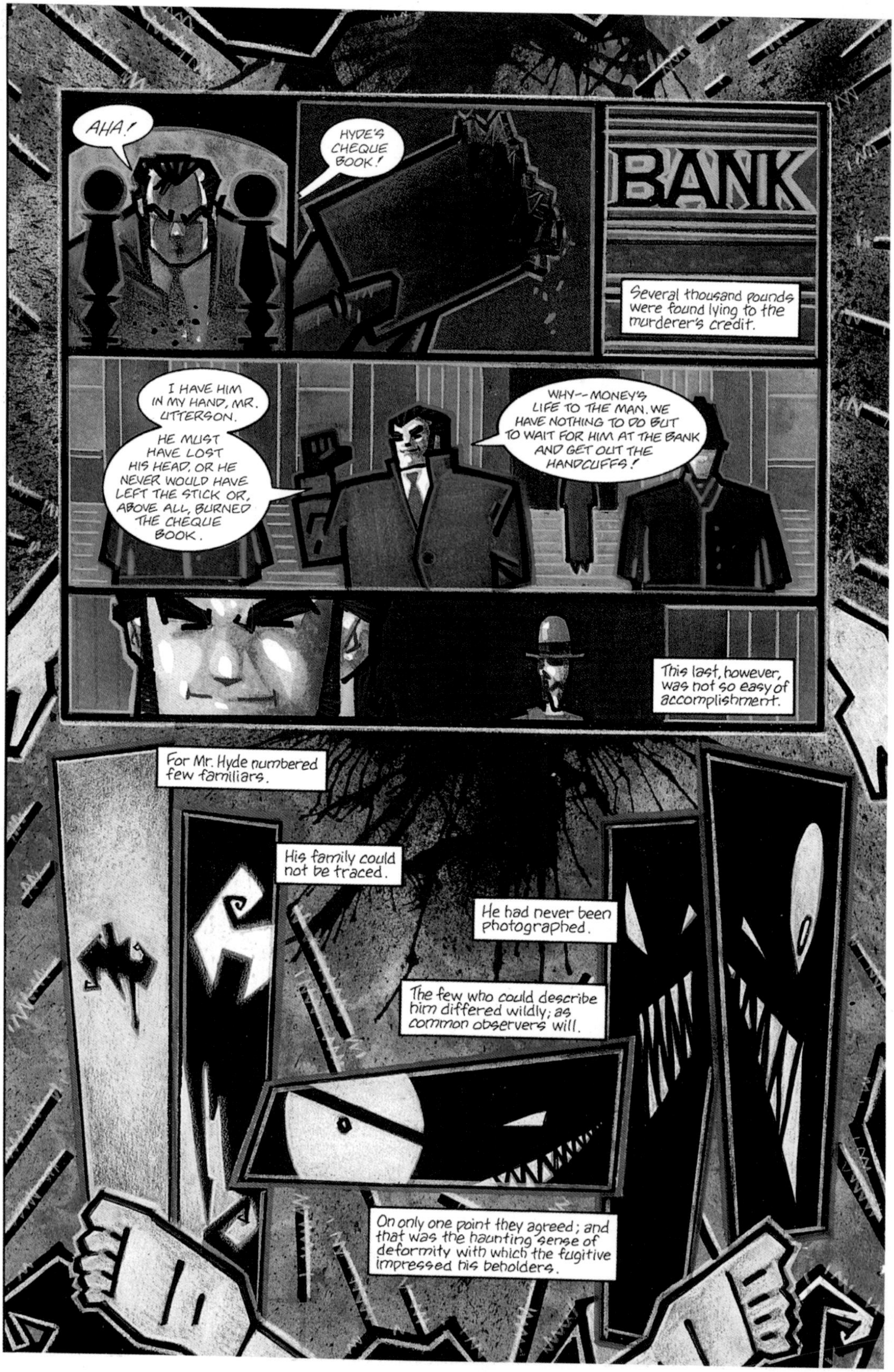

AHA!
HYDE'S CHEQUE BOOK!
BANK
Several thousand pounds were found lying to the murderer's credit.
I HAVE HIM IN MY HAND, MR. UTTERSON.
HE MUST HAVE LOST HIS HEAD, OR HE NEVER WOULD HAVE LEFT THE STICK OR, ABOVE ALL, BURNED THE CHEQUE BOOK.
WHY--MONEY'S LIFE TO THE MAN. WE HAVE NOTHING TO DO BUT TO WAIT FOR HIM AT THE BANK AND GET OUT THE HANDCUFFS!
This last, however, was not so easy of accomplishment.
For Mr. Hyde numbered few familiars.
His family could not be traced.
He had never been photographed.
The few who could describe him differed wildly; as common observers will.
On only one point they agreed; and that was the haunting sense of deformity with which the fugitive impressed his beholders.

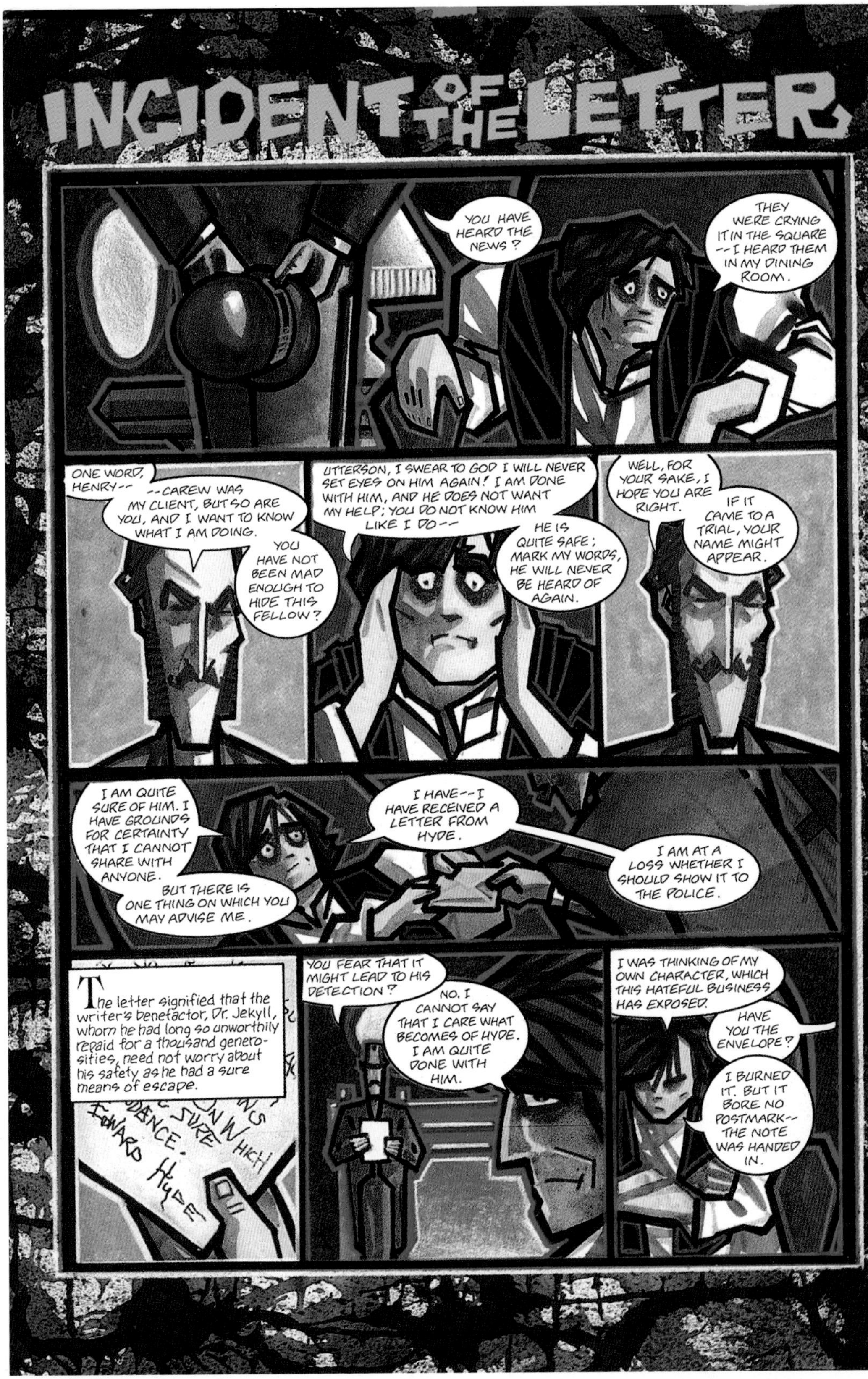
INCIDENT OF THE LETTER
YOU HAVE HEARD THE NEWS?
THEY WERE CRYING IT IN THE SQUARE --I HEARD THEM IN MY DINING ROOM.
ONE WORD, HENRY--
--CAREW WAS MY CLIENT, BUT SO ARE YOU, AND I WANT TO KNOW WHAT I AM DOING.
YOU HAVE NOT BEEN MAD ENOUGH TO HIDE THIS FELLOW?
UTTERSON, I SWEAR TO GOD I WILL NEVER SET EYES ON HIM AGAIN! I AM DONE WITH HIM, AND HE DOES NOT WANT MY HELP; YOU DO NOT KNOW HIM LIKE I DO--
HE IS QUITE SAFE; MARK MY WORDS, HE WILL NEVER BE HEARD OF AGAIN.
WELL, FOR YOUR SAKE, I HOPE YOU ARE RIGHT.
IF IT CAME TO A TRIAL, YOUR NAME MIGHT APPEAR.
I AM QUITE SURE OF HIM. I HAVE GROUNDS FOR CERTAINTY THAT I CANNOT SHARE WITH ANYONE.
BUT THERE IS ONE THING ON WHICH YOU MAY ADVISE ME.
I HAVE--I HAVE RECEIVED A LETTER FROM HYDE.
I AM AT A LOSS WHETHER I SHOULD SHOW IT TO THE POLICE.
The letter signified that the writer's benefactor, Dr. Jekyll, whom he had long so unworthily repaid for a thousand generosities, need not worry about his safety as he had a sure means of escape.
YOU FEAR THAT IT MIGHT LEAD TO HIS DETECTION?
NO. I CANNOT SAY THAT I CARE WHAT BECOMES OF HYDE. I AM QUITE DONE WITH HIM.
I WAS THINKING OF MY OWN CHARACTER, WHICH THIS HATEFUL BUSINESS HAS EXPOSED.
HAVE YOU THE ENVELOPE?
I BURNED IT. BUT IT BORE NO POSTMARK-- THE NOTE WAS HANDED IN.

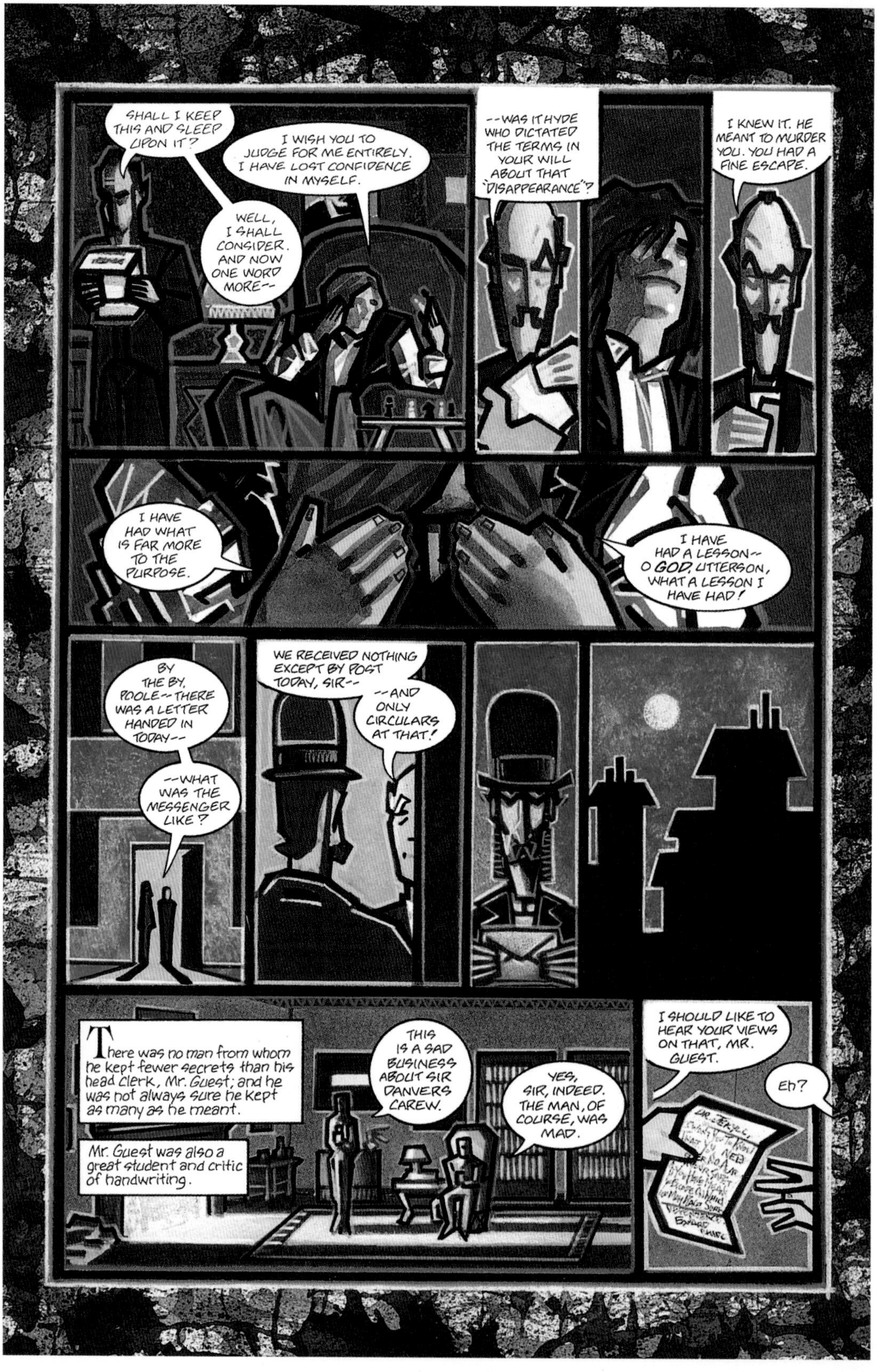
SHALL I KEEP THIS AND SLEEP UPON IT?
I WISH YOU TO JUDGE FOR ME ENTIRELY. I HAVE LOST CONFIDENCE IN MYSELF.
WELL, I SHALL CONSIDER. AND NOW ONE WORD MORE--
--WAS IT HYDE WHO DICTATED THE TERMS IN YOUR WILL ABOUT THAT "DISAPPEARANCE"?
I KNEW IT. HE MEANT TO MURDER YOU. YOU HAD A FINE ESCAPE.
I HAVE HAD WHAT IS FAR MORE TO THE PURPOSE.
I HAVE HAD A LESSON-- O GOD, UTTERSON, WHAT A LESSON I HAVE HAD!
BY THE BY, POOLE--THERE WAS A LETTER HANDED IN TODAY--
--WHAT WAS THE MESSENGER LIKE?
WE RECEIVED NOTHING EXCEPT BY POST TODAY, SIR--
--AND ONLY CIRCULARS AT THAT!
There was no man from whom he kept fewer secrets than his head clerk, Mr. Guest; and he was not always sure he kept as many as he meant.
Mr. Guest was also a great student and critic of handwriting.
THIS IS A SAD BUSINESS ABOUT SIR DANVERS CAREW.
YES, SIR, INDEED. THE MAN, OF COURSE, WAS MAD.
I SHOULD LIKE TO HEAR YOUR VIEWS ON THAT, MR. GUEST.
Eh?

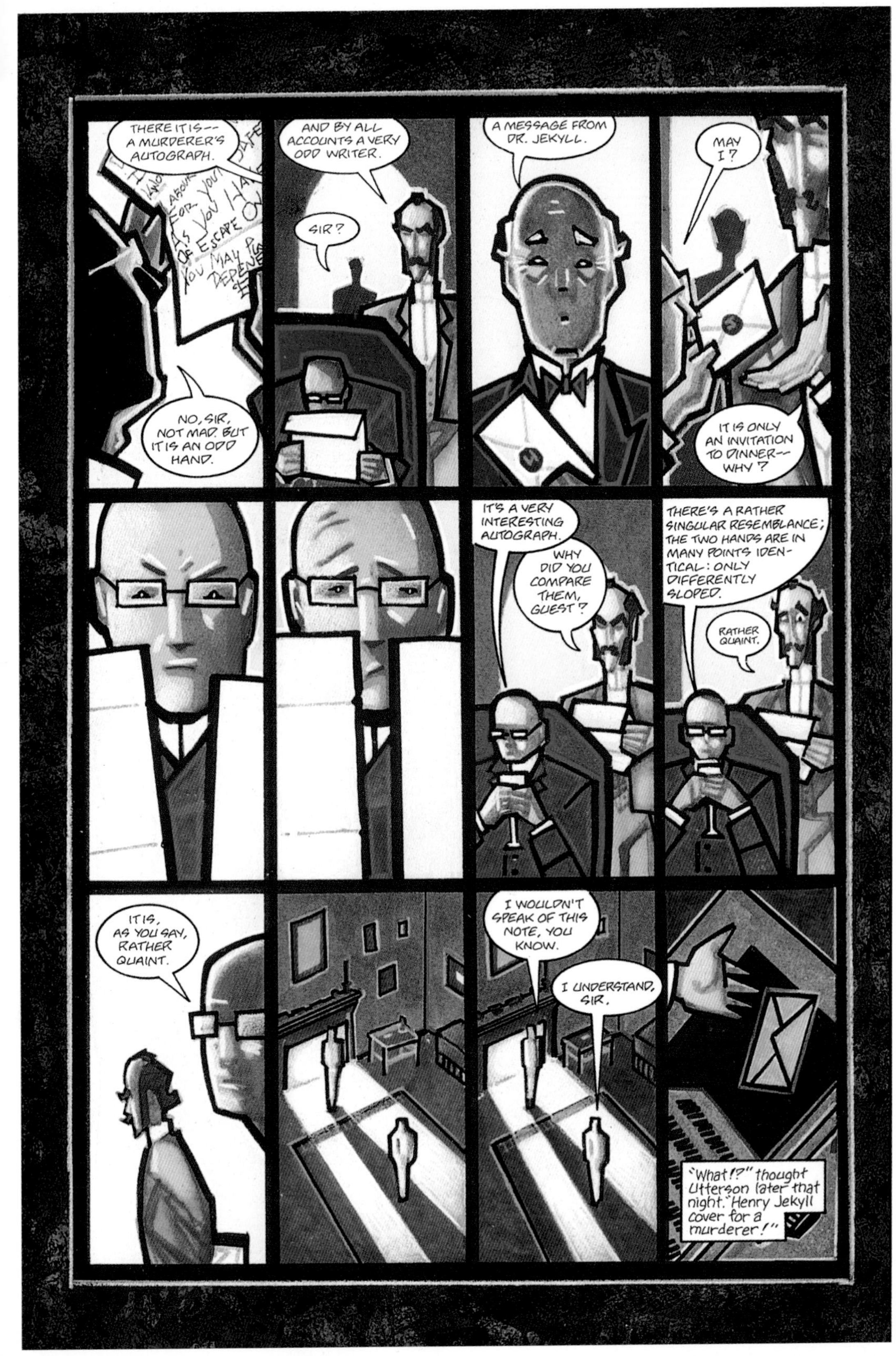
THERE IT IS-- A MURDERER'S AUTOGRAPH.
NO, SIR, NOT MAD. BUT IT IS AN ODD HAND.
AND BY ALL ACCOUNTS A VERY ODD WRITER.
SIR?
A MESSAGE FROM DR. JEKYLL.
MAY I?
IT IS ONLY AN INVITATION TO DINNER-- WHY?
IT'S A VERY INTERESTING AUTOGRAPH.
WHY DID YOU COMPARE THEM, GUEST?
THERE'S A RATHER SINGULAR RESEMBLANCE; THE TWO HANDS ARE IN MANY POINTS IDENTICAL: ONLY DIFFERENTLY SLOPED.
RATHER QUAINT.
IT IS, AS YOU SAY, RATHER QUAINT.
I WOULDN'T SPEAK OF THIS NOTE, YOU KNOW.
I UNDERSTAND, SIR.
"What!?" thought Utterson later that night. "Henry Jekyll cover for a murderer!"

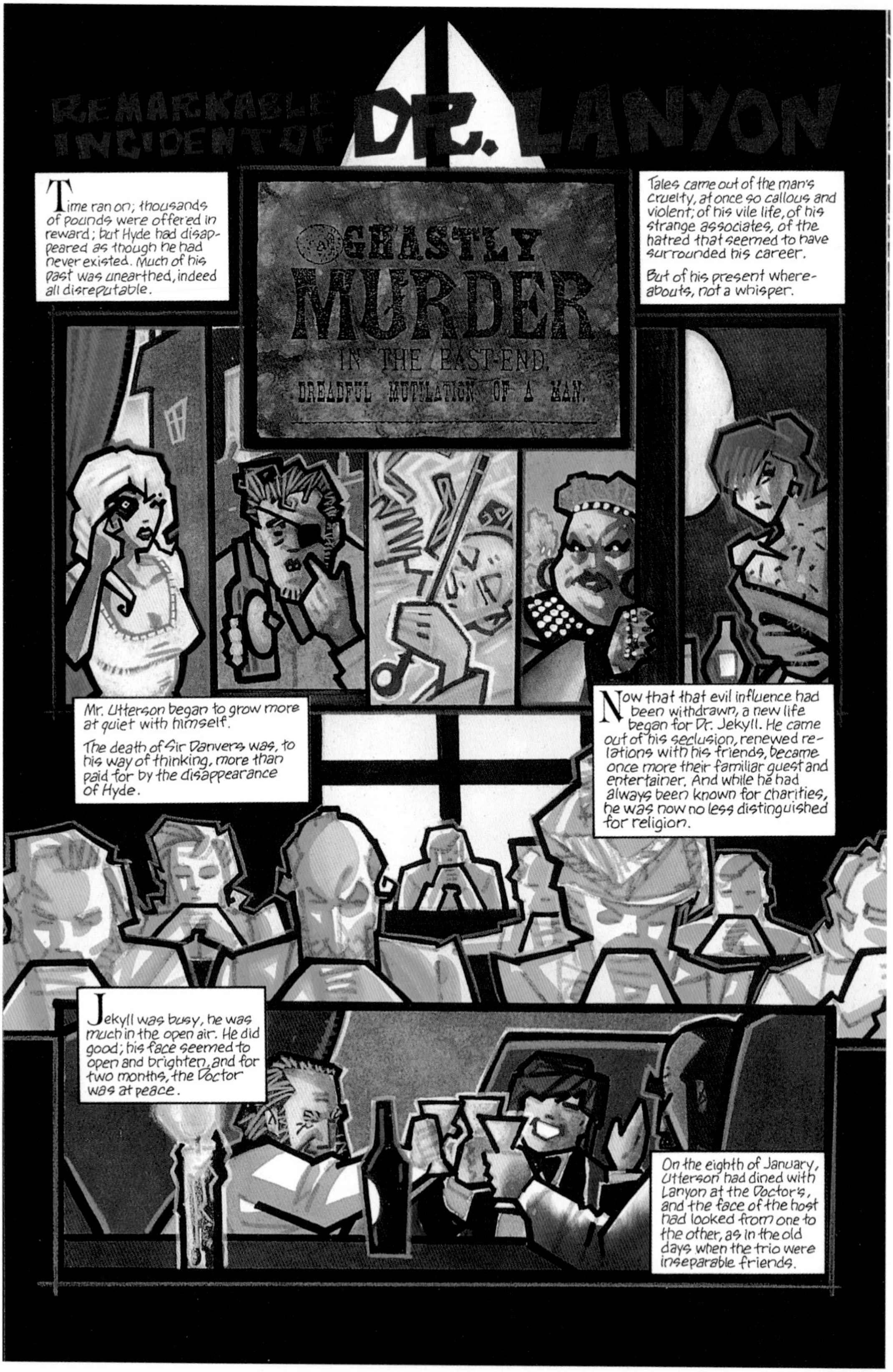
REMARKABLE INCIDENT OF DR. LANYON
Time ran on; thousands of pounds were offered in reward; but Hyde had disappeared as though he had never existed. Much of his past was unearthed, indeed all disreputable.
GHASTLY MURDER IN THE EAST-END. DREADFUL MUTILATION OF A MAN.
Tales came out of the man's cruelty, at once so callous and violent; of his vile life, of his strange associates, of the hatred that seemed to have surrounded his career.
But of his present whereabouts, not a whisper.
Mr. Utterson began to grow more at quiet with himself.
The death of Sir Danvers was, to his way of thinking, more than paid for by the disappearance of Hyde.
Now that that evil influence had been withdrawn, a new life began for Dr. Jekyll. He came out of his seclusion, renewed relations with his friends, became once more their familiar guest and entertainer. And while he had always been known for charities, he was now no less distinguished for religion.
Jekyll was busy, he was much in the open air. He did good; his face seemed to open and brighten, and for two months, the Doctor was at peace.
On the eighth of January, Utterson had dined with Lanyon at the Doctor's, and the face of the host had looked from one to the other, as in the old days when the trio were inseparable friends.

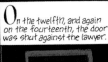    

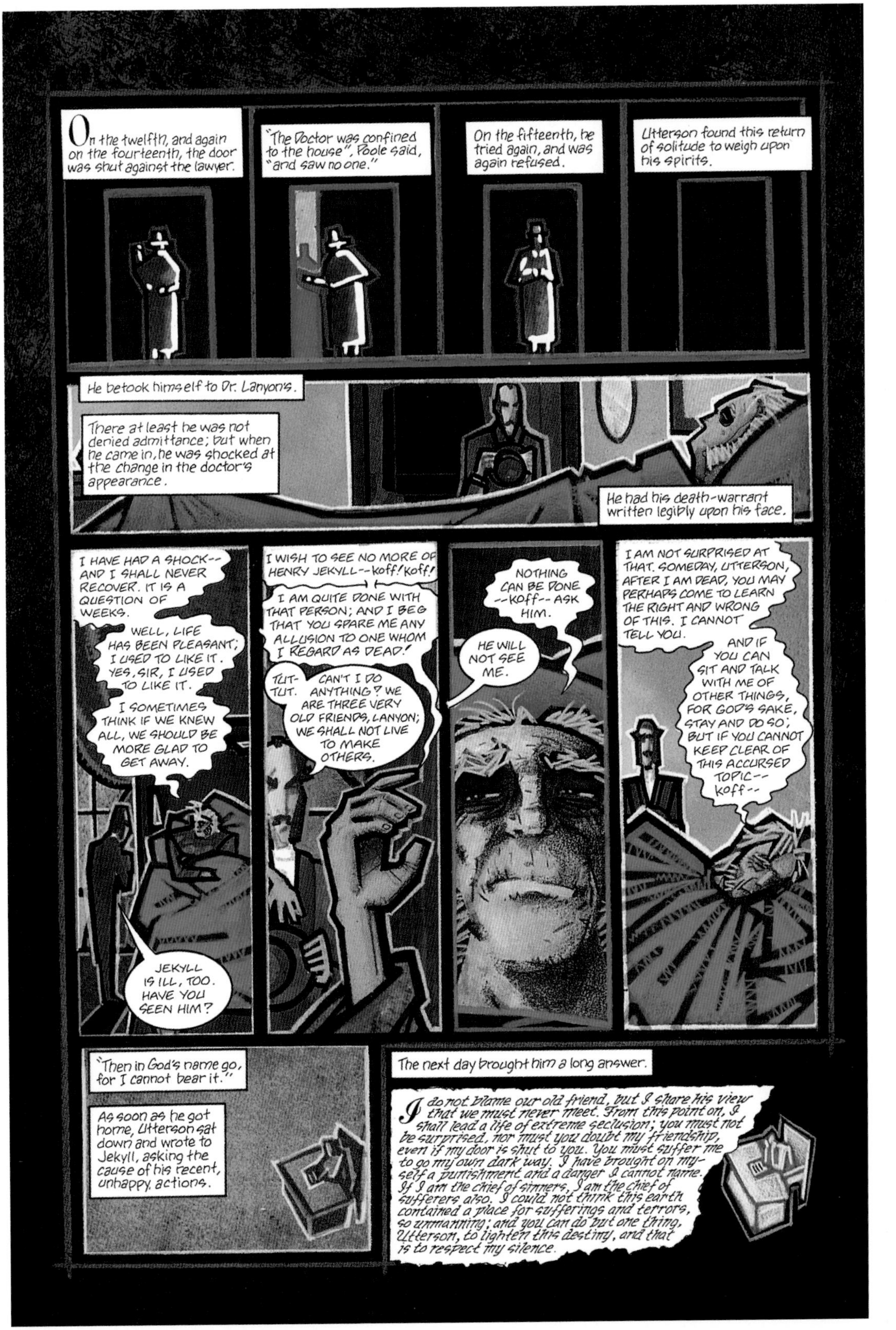

On the twelfth, and again on the fourteenth, the door was shut against the lawyer.

"The Doctor was confined to the house", Poole said, "and saw no one."

On the fifteenth, he tried again, and was again refused.

Utterson found this return of solitude to weigh upon his spirits.

He betook himself to Dr. Lanyon's.

There at least he was not denied admittance; but when he came in, he was shocked at the change in the doctor's appearance.

He had his death-warrant written legibly upon his face.

I HAVE HAD A SHOCK-- AND I SHALL NEVER RECOVER. IT IS A QUESTION OF WEEKS.

WELL, LIFE HAS BEEN PLEASANT; I USED TO LIKE IT. YES, SIR, I USED TO LIKE IT.

I SOMETIMES THINK IF WE KNEW ALL, WE SHOULD BE MORE GLAD TO GET AWAY.

JEKYLL IS ILL, TOO. HAVE YOU SEEN HIM?

I WISH TO SEE NO MORE OF HENRY JEKYLL--koff! koff!

I AM QUITE DONE WITH THAT PERSON; AND I BEG THAT YOU SPARE ME ANY ALLUSION TO ONE WHOM I REGARD AS DEAD!

TUT- TUT. CAN'T I DO ANYTHING? WE ARE THREE VERY OLD FRIENDS, LANYON; WE SHALL NOT LIVE TO MAKE OTHERS.

NOTHING CAN BE DONE --koff-- ASK HIM.

HE WILL NOT SEE ME.

I AM NOT SURPRISED AT THAT. SOMEDAY, UTTERSON, AFTER I AM DEAD, YOU MAY PERHAPS COME TO LEARN THE RIGHT AND WRONG OF THIS. I CANNOT TELL YOU.

AND IF YOU CAN SIT AND TALK WITH ME OF OTHER THINGS, FOR GOD'S SAKE, STAY AND DO SO; BUT IF YOU CANNOT KEEP CLEAR OF THIS ACCURSED TOPIC-- koff--

"Then in God's name go, for I cannot bear it."

As soon as he got home, Utterson sat down and wrote to Jekyll, asking the cause of his recent, unhappy, actions.

The next day brought him a long answer.

I do not blame our old friend, but I share his view that we must never meet. From this point on, I shall lead a life of extreme seclusion; you must not be surprised, nor must you doubt my friendship, even if my door is shut to you. You must suffer me to go my own dark way. I have brought on myself a punishment and a danger I cannot name. If I am the chief of sinners, I am the chief of sufferers also. I could not think this earth contained a place for sufferings and terrors, so unmanning; and you can do but one thing, Utterson, to lighten this destiny, and that is to respect my silence.

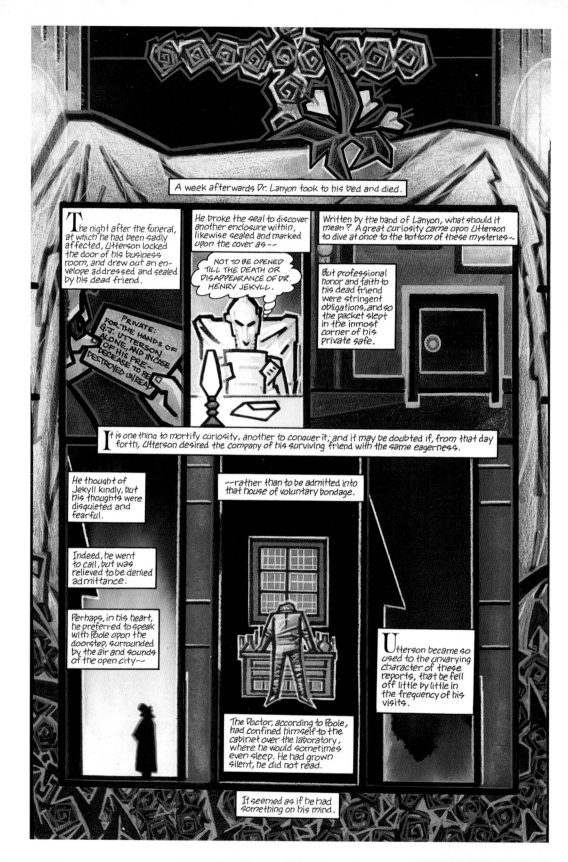

A week afterwards Dr. Lanyon took to his bed and died.

The night after the funeral, at which he had been sadly affected, Utterson locked the door of his business room, and drew out an envelope addressed and sealed by his dead friend.

PRIVATE: FOR THE HANDS OF G.J. UTTERSON ALONE, AND IN CASE OF HIS PRE-DECEASE TO BE DESTROYED UNREAD.

He broke the seal to discover another enclosure within, likewise sealed and marked upon the cover as--

NOT TO BE OPENED TILL THE DEATH OR DISAPPEARANCE OF DR. HENRY JEKYLL.

Written by the hand of Lanyon, what should it mean? A great curiosity came upon Utterson to dive at once to the bottom of these mysteries--

But professional honor and faith to his dead friend were stringent obligations, and so the packet slept in the inmost corner of his private safe.

It is one thing to mortify curiosity, another to conquer it; and it may be doubted if, from that day forth, Utterson desired the company of his surviving friend with the same eagerness.

He thought of Jekyll kindly, but his thoughts were disquieted and fearful.

Indeed, he went to call, but was relieved to be denied admittance.

Perhaps, in his heart, he preferred to speak with Poole upon the doorstep, surrounded by the air and sounds of the open city--

--rather than to be admitted into that house of voluntary bondage.

The Doctor, according to Poole, had confined himself to the cabinet over the laboratory, where he would sometimes even sleep. He had grown silent, he did not read.

Utterson became so used to the unvarying character of these reports, that he fell off little by little in the frequency of his visits.

It seemed as if he had something on his mind.

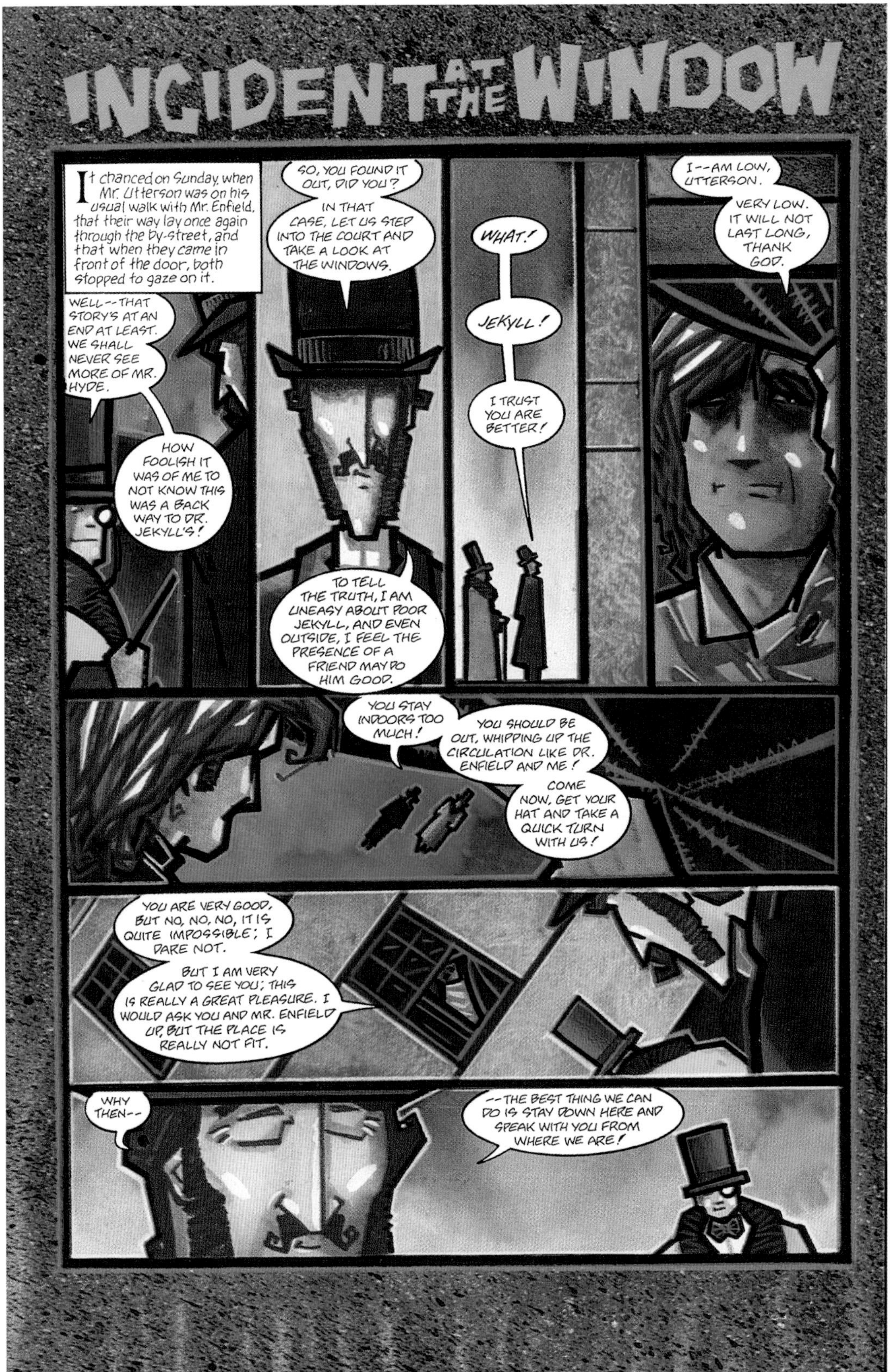
INCIDENT AT THE WINDOW
It chanced on Sunday, when Mr. Utterson was on his usual walk with Mr. Enfield, that their way lay once again through the by-street, and that when they came in front of the door, both stopped to gaze on it.
WELL--THAT STORY'S AT AN END AT LEAST. WE SHALL NEVER SEE MORE OF MR. HYDE.
HOW FOOLISH IT WAS OF ME TO NOT KNOW THIS WAS A BACK WAY TO DR. JEKYLL'S!
SO, YOU FOUND IT OUT, DID YOU?
IN THAT CASE, LET US STEP INTO THE COURT AND TAKE A LOOK AT THE WINDOWS.
TO TELL THE TRUTH, I AM UNEASY ABOUT POOR JEKYLL, AND EVEN OUTSIDE, I FEEL THE PRESENCE OF A FRIEND MAY DO HIM GOOD.
WHAT!
JEKYLL!
I TRUST YOU ARE BETTER!
I--AM LOW, UTTERSON.
VERY LOW. IT WILL NOT LAST LONG, THANK GOD.
YOU STAY INDOORS TOO MUCH!
YOU SHOULD BE OUT, WHIPPING UP THE CIRCULATION LIKE DR. ENFIELD AND ME!
COME NOW, GET YOUR HAT AND TAKE A QUICK TURN WITH US!
YOU ARE VERY GOOD, BUT NO, NO, NO, IT IS QUITE IMPOSSIBLE; I DARE NOT.
BUT I AM VERY GLAD TO SEE YOU; THIS IS REALLY A GREAT PLEASURE. I WOULD ASK YOU AND MR. ENFIELD UP, BUT THE PLACE IS REALLY NOT FIT.
WHY THEN--
--THE BEST THING WE CAN DO IS STAY DOWN HERE AND SPEAK WITH YOU FROM WHERE WE ARE!

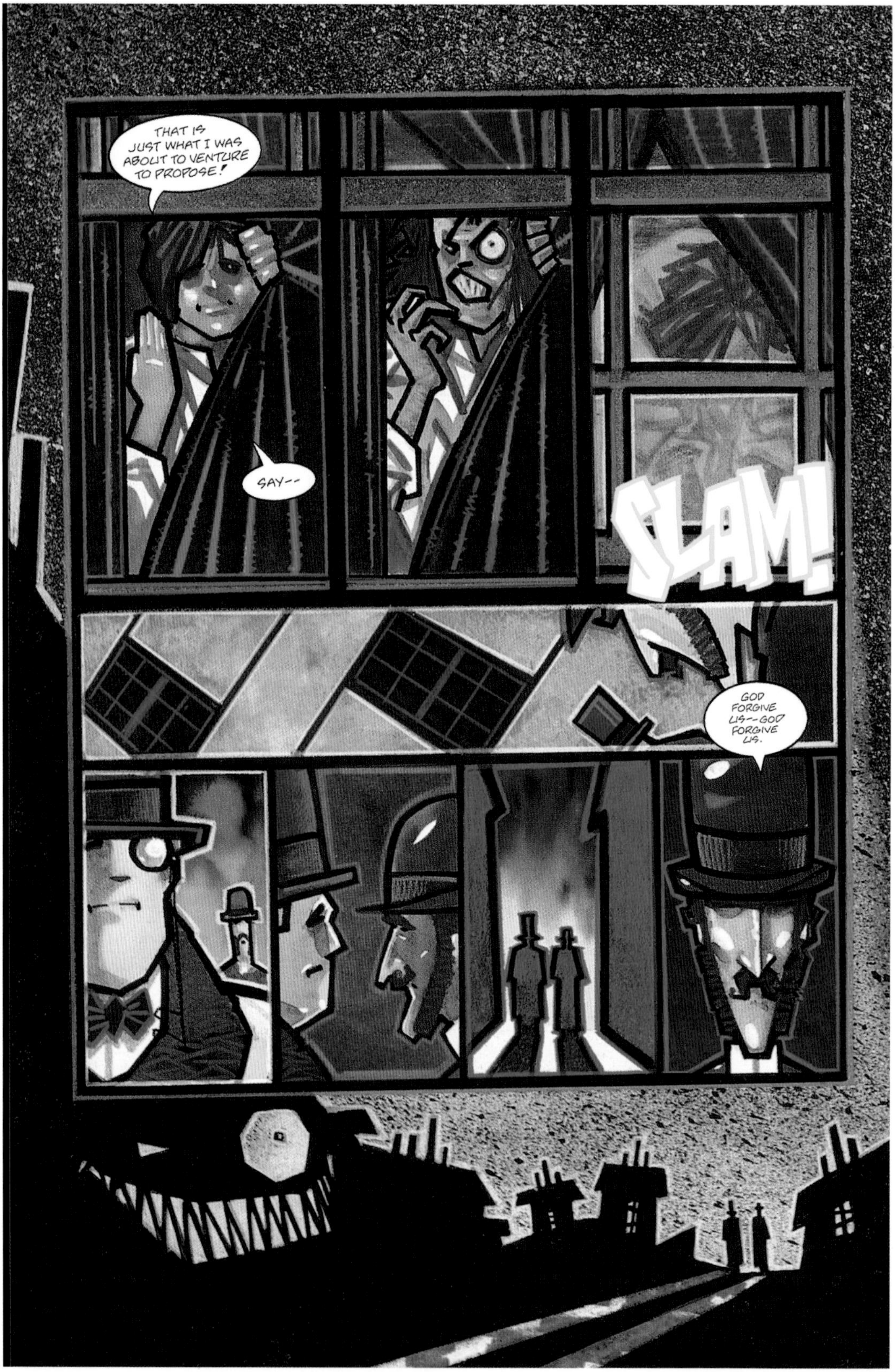
THAT IS JUST WHAT I WAS ABOUT TO VENTURE TO PROPOSE!
SAY--
SLAM!
GOD FORGIVE US--GOD FORGIVE US.

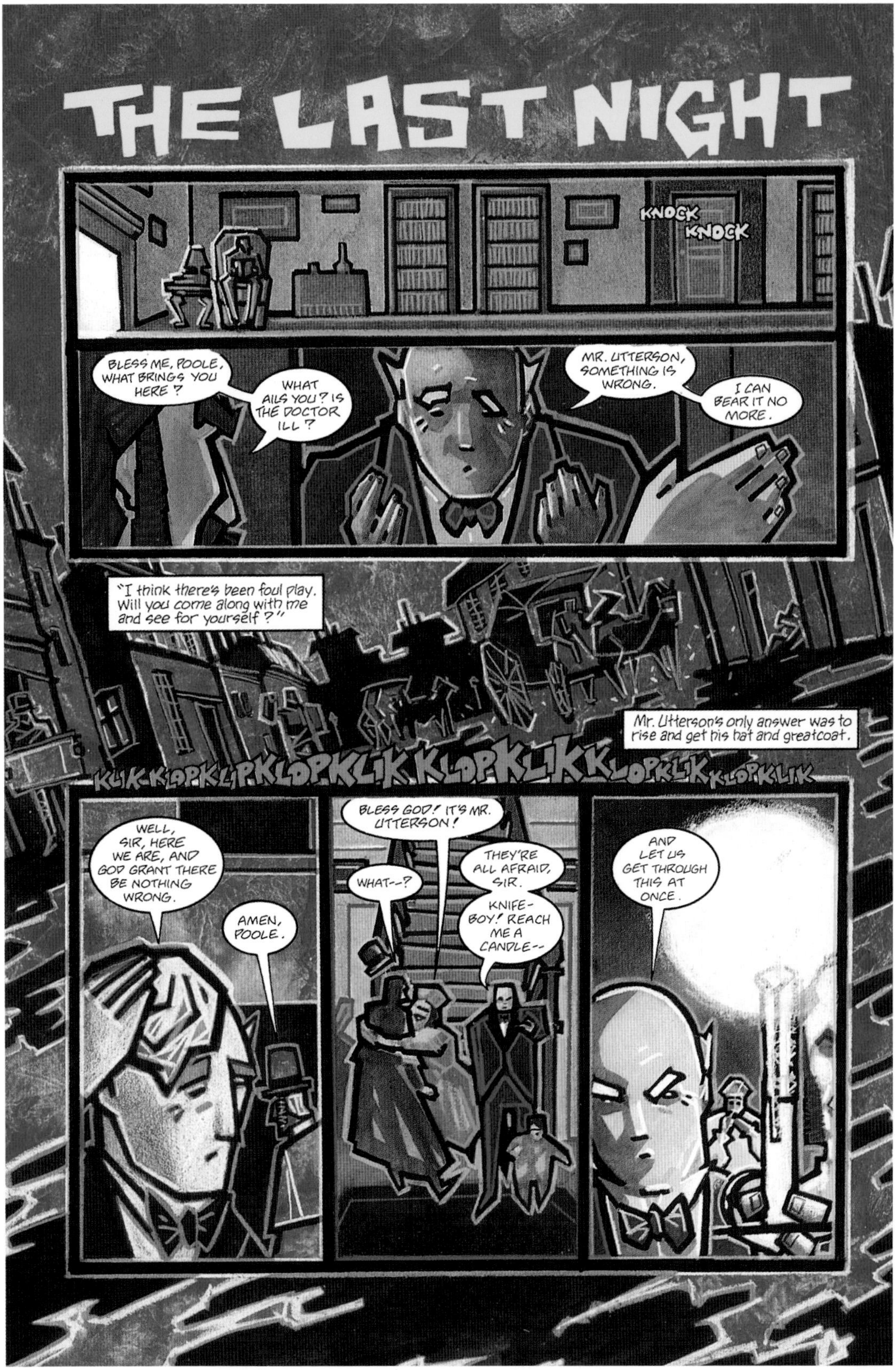
THE LAST NIGHT
KNOCK KNOCK
BLESS ME, POOLE, WHAT BRINGS YOU HERE?
WHAT AILS YOU? IS THE DOCTOR ILL?
MR. UTTERSON, SOMETHING IS WRONG.
I CAN BEAR IT NO MORE.
"I think there's been foul play. Will you come along with me and see for yourself?"
Mr. Utterson's only answer was to rise and get his hat and greatcoat.
KLIK-KLOPKLIPKLOPKLIKKLOPKLIKKLOPKLIKKLOPKLIK
WELL, SIR, HERE WE ARE, AND GOD GRANT THERE BE NOTHING WRONG.
AMEN, POOLE.
BLESS GOD! IT'S MR. UTTERSON!
WHAT--?
THEY'RE ALL AFRAID, SIR.
KNIFE-BOY! REACH ME A CANDLE--
AND LET US GET THROUGH THIS AT ONCE.

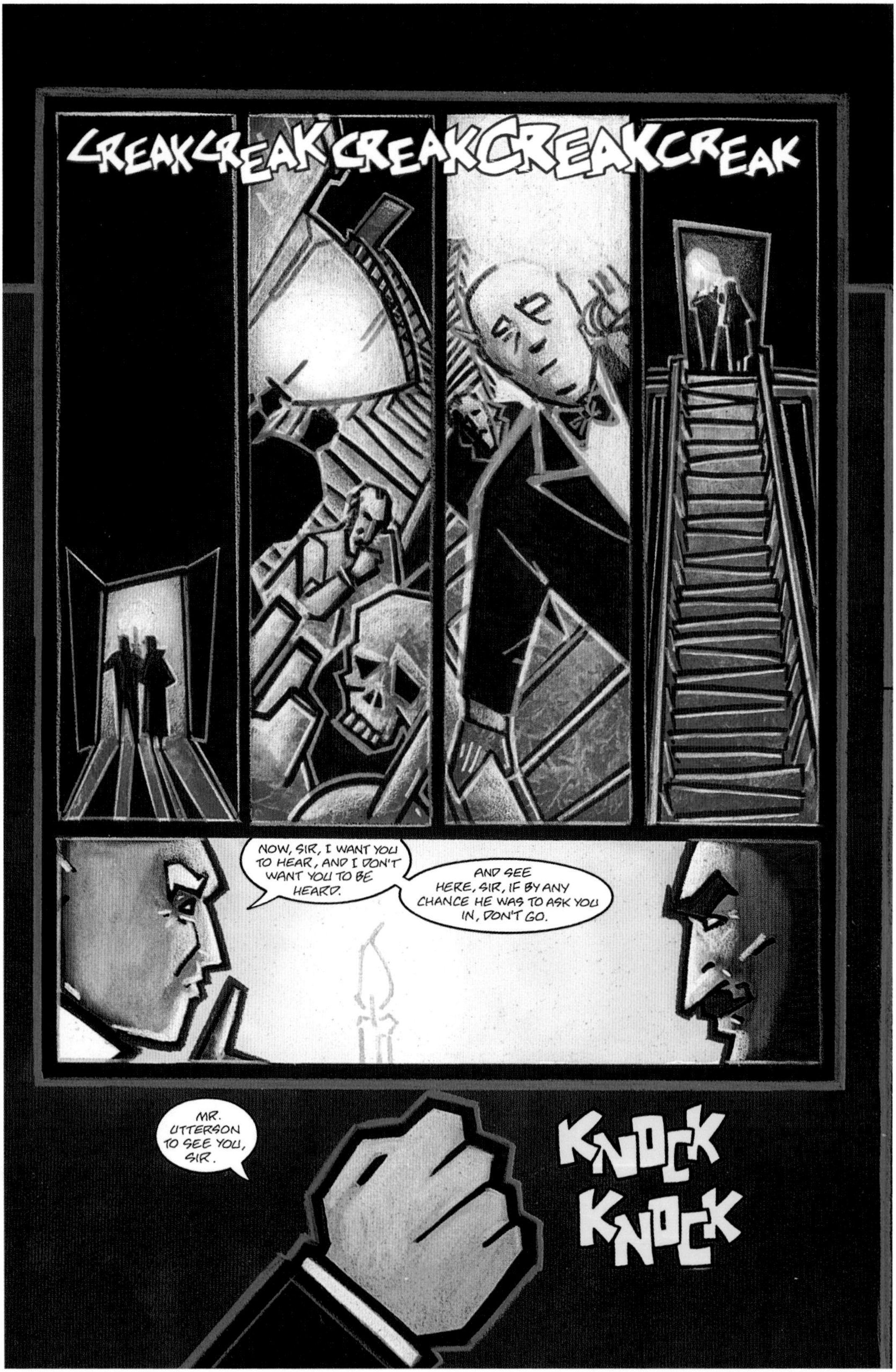
CREAKCREAKCREAKCREAKCREAK
NOW, SIR, I WANT YOU TO HEAR, AND I DON'T WANT YOU TO BE HEARD.
AND SEE HERE, SIR, IF BY ANY CHANCE HE WAS TO ASK YOU IN, DON'T GO.
MR. UTTERSON TO SEE YOU, SIR.
KNOCK KNOCK

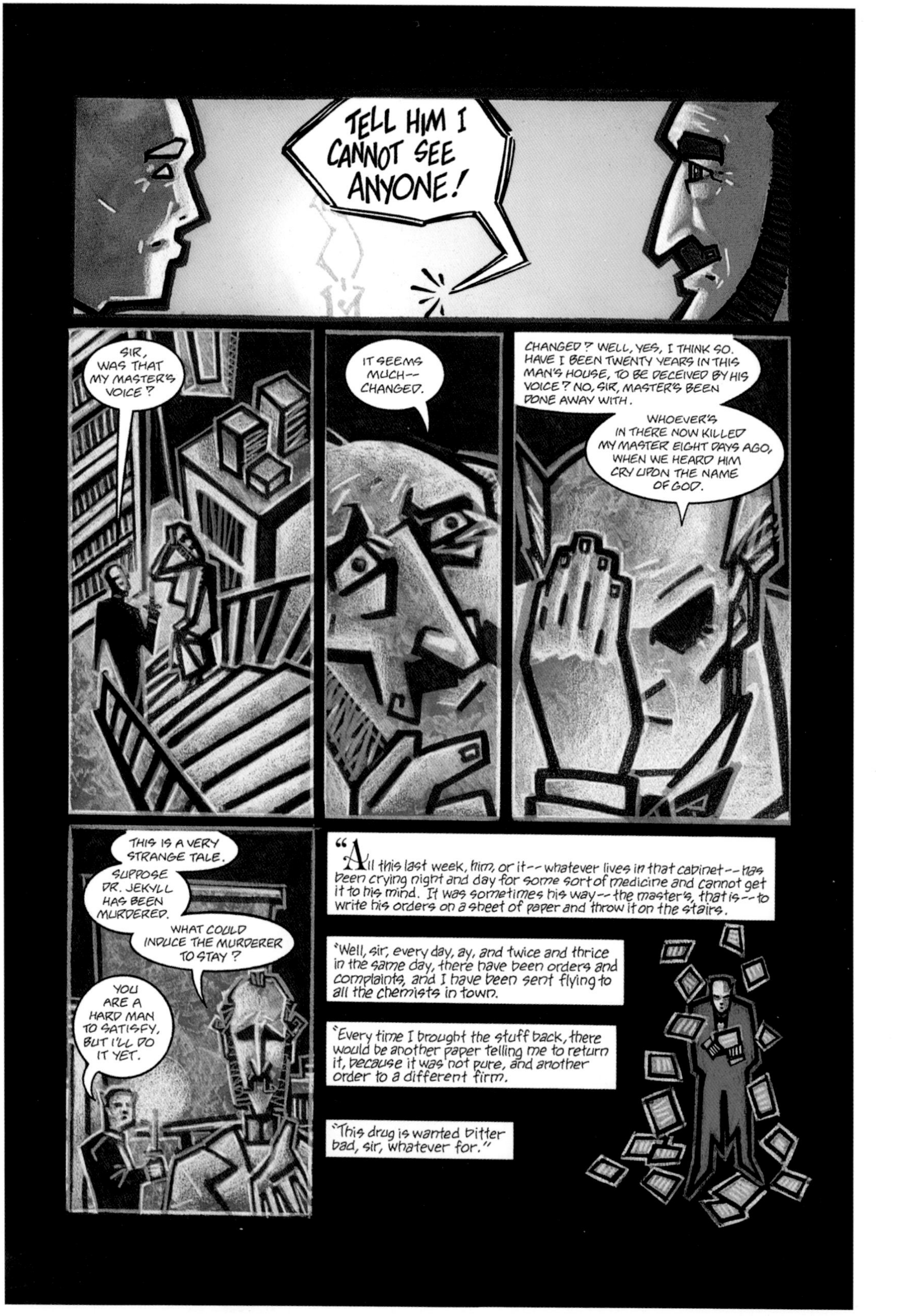
TELL HIM I CANNOT SEE ANYONE!
SIR, WAS THAT MY MASTER'S VOICE?
IT SEEMS MUCH-- CHANGED.
CHANGED? WELL, YES, I THINK SO. HAVE I BEEN TWENTY YEARS IN THIS MAN'S HOUSE, TO BE DECEIVED BY HIS VOICE? NO, SIR, MASTER'S BEEN DONE AWAY WITH.
WHOEVER'S IN THERE NOW KILLED MY MASTER EIGHT DAYS AGO, WHEN WE HEARD HIM CRY UPON THE NAME OF GOD.
THIS IS A VERY STRANGE TALE.
SUPPOSE DR. JEKYLL HAS BEEN MURDERED.
WHAT COULD INDUCE THE MURDERER TO STAY?
YOU ARE A HARD MAN TO SATISFY, BUT I'LL DO IT YET.
"All this last week, him, or it-- whatever lives in that cabinet-- has been crying night and day for some sort of medicine and cannot get it to his mind. It was sometimes his way-- the master's, that is-- to write his orders on a sheet of paper and throw it on the stairs.
"Well, sir, every day, ay, and twice and thrice in the same day, there have been orders and complaints, and I have been sent flying to all the chemists in town.
"Every time I brought the stuff back, there would be another paper telling me to return it, because it was not pure, and another order to a different firm.
"This drug is wanted bitter bad, sir, whatever for."

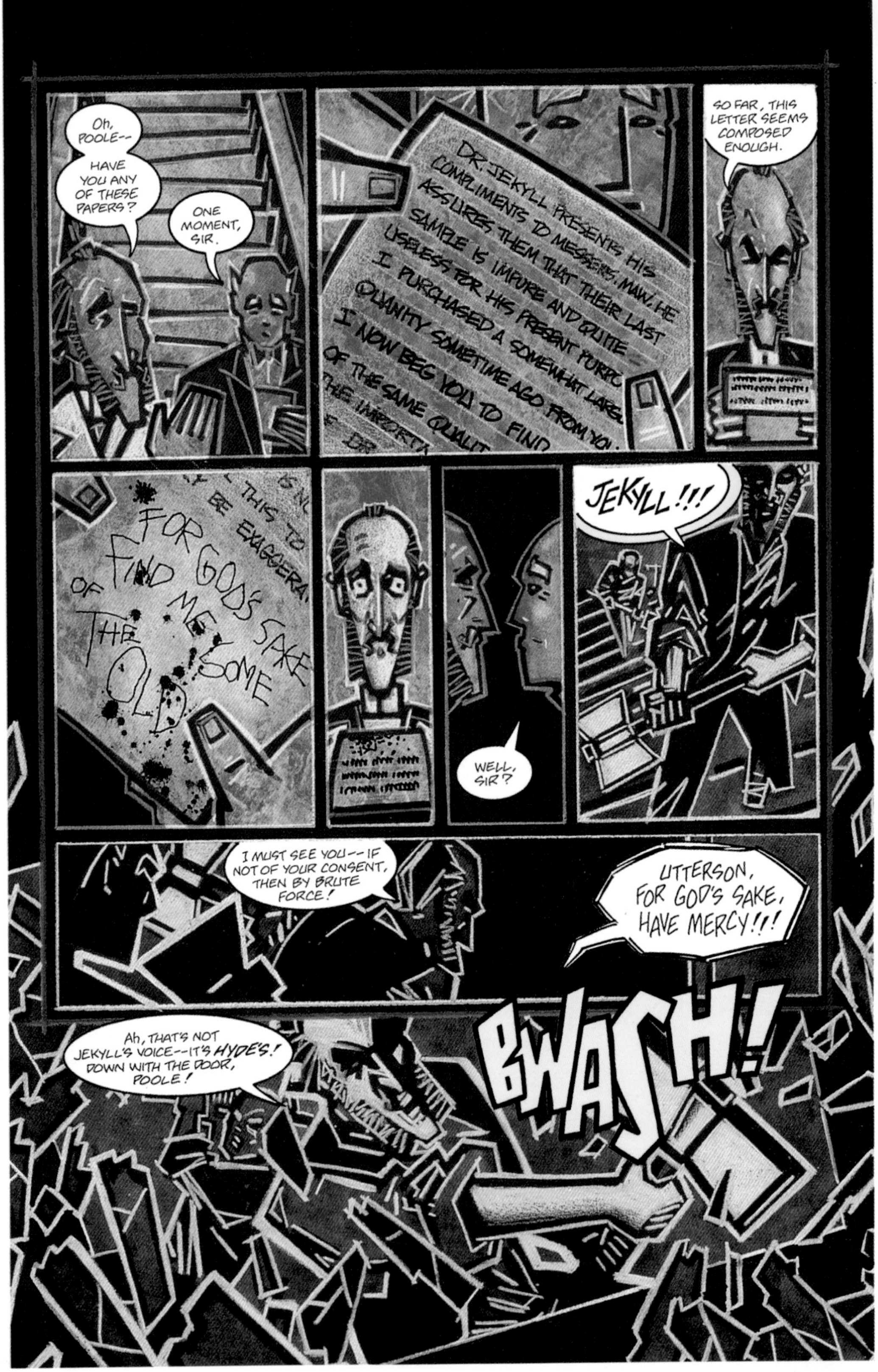
Oh, POOLE--
HAVE YOU ANY OF THESE PAPERS?
ONE MOMENT, SIR.
DR. JEKYLL PRESENTS HIS
COMPLIMENTS TO MESSERS. MAW. HE
ASSURES THEM THAT THEIR LAST
SAMPLE IS IMPURE AND QUITE
USELESS FOR HIS PRESENT PURPO
I PURCHASED A SOMEWHAT LARG
QUANITY SOMETIME AGO FROM YO
I NOW BEG YOU TO FIND
OF THE SAME QUALIT
SO FAR, THIS LETTER SEEMS COMPOSED ENOUGH.
THIS TO
BE EXAGGERA
FOR GOD'S SAKE
FIND ME SOME
OF THE OLD
WELL, SIR?
JEKYLL!!!
I MUST SEE YOU-- IF NOT OF YOUR CONSENT, THEN BY BRUTE FORCE!
UTTERSON, FOR GOD'S SAKE, HAVE MERCY!!!
BWASH!
Ah, THAT'S NOT JEKYLL'S VOICE--IT'S HYDE'S! DOWN WITH THE DOOR, POOLE!

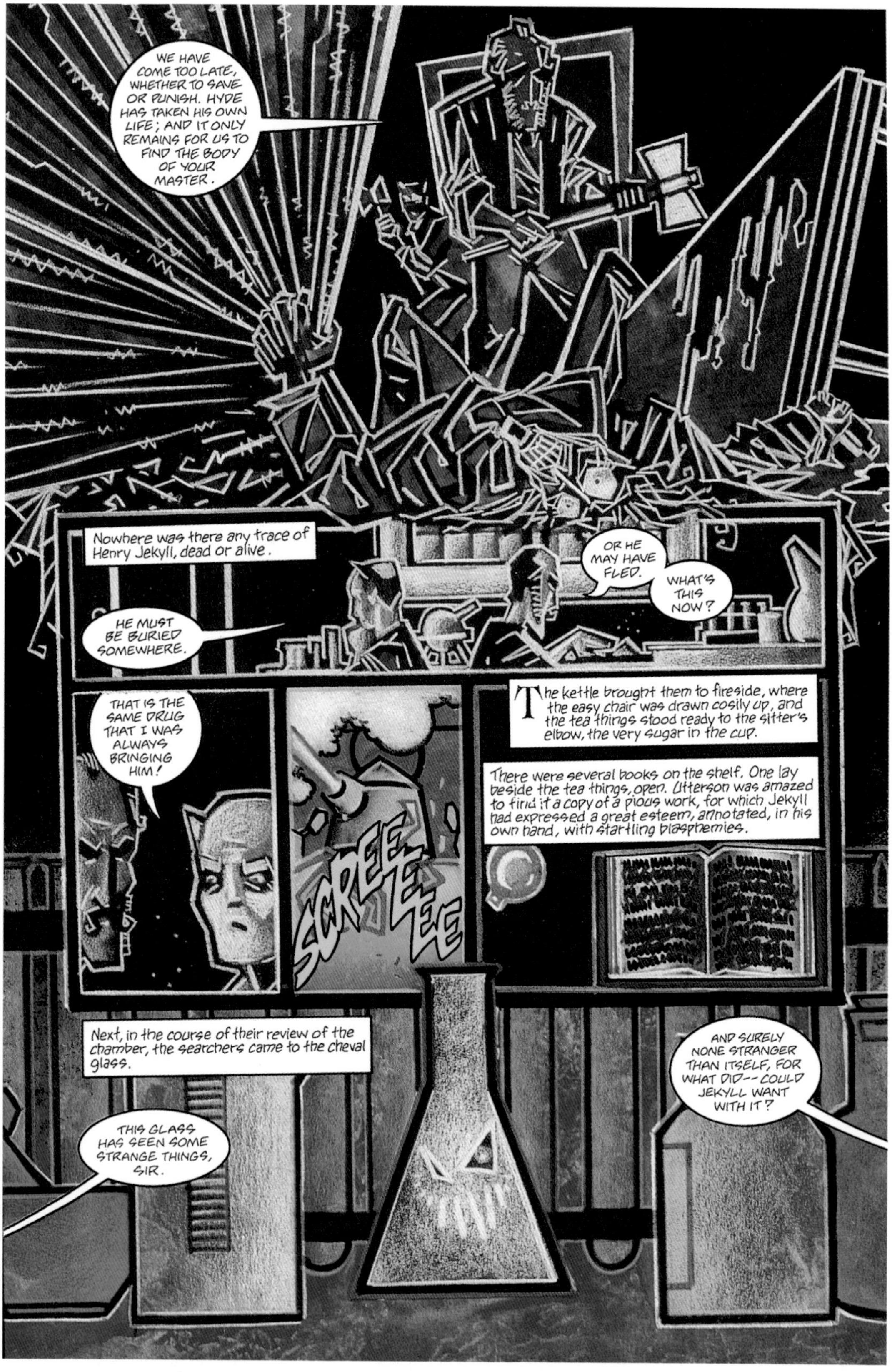
WE HAVE COME TOO LATE, WHETHER TO SAVE OR PUNISH. HYDE HAS TAKEN HIS OWN LIFE; AND IT ONLY REMAINS FOR US TO FIND THE BODY OF YOUR MASTER.
Nowhere was there any trace of Henry Jekyll, dead or alive.
HE MUST BE BURIED SOMEWHERE.
OR HE MAY HAVE FLED.
WHAT'S THIS NOW?
THAT IS THE SAME DRUG THAT I WAS ALWAYS BRINGING HIM!
SCREEEEEE
The kettle brought them to fireside, where the easy chair was drawn cosily up, and the tea things stood ready to the sitter's elbow, the very sugar in the cup.
There were several books on the shelf. One lay beside the tea things, open. Utterson was amazed to find it a copy of a pious work, for which Jekyll had expressed a great esteem, annotated, in his own hand, with startling blasphemies.
Next, in the course of their review of the chamber, the searchers came to the cheval glass.
THIS GLASS HAS SEEN SOME STRANGE THINGS, SIR.
AND SURELY NONE STRANGER THAN ITSELF, FOR WHAT DID-- COULD JEKYLL WANT WITH IT?

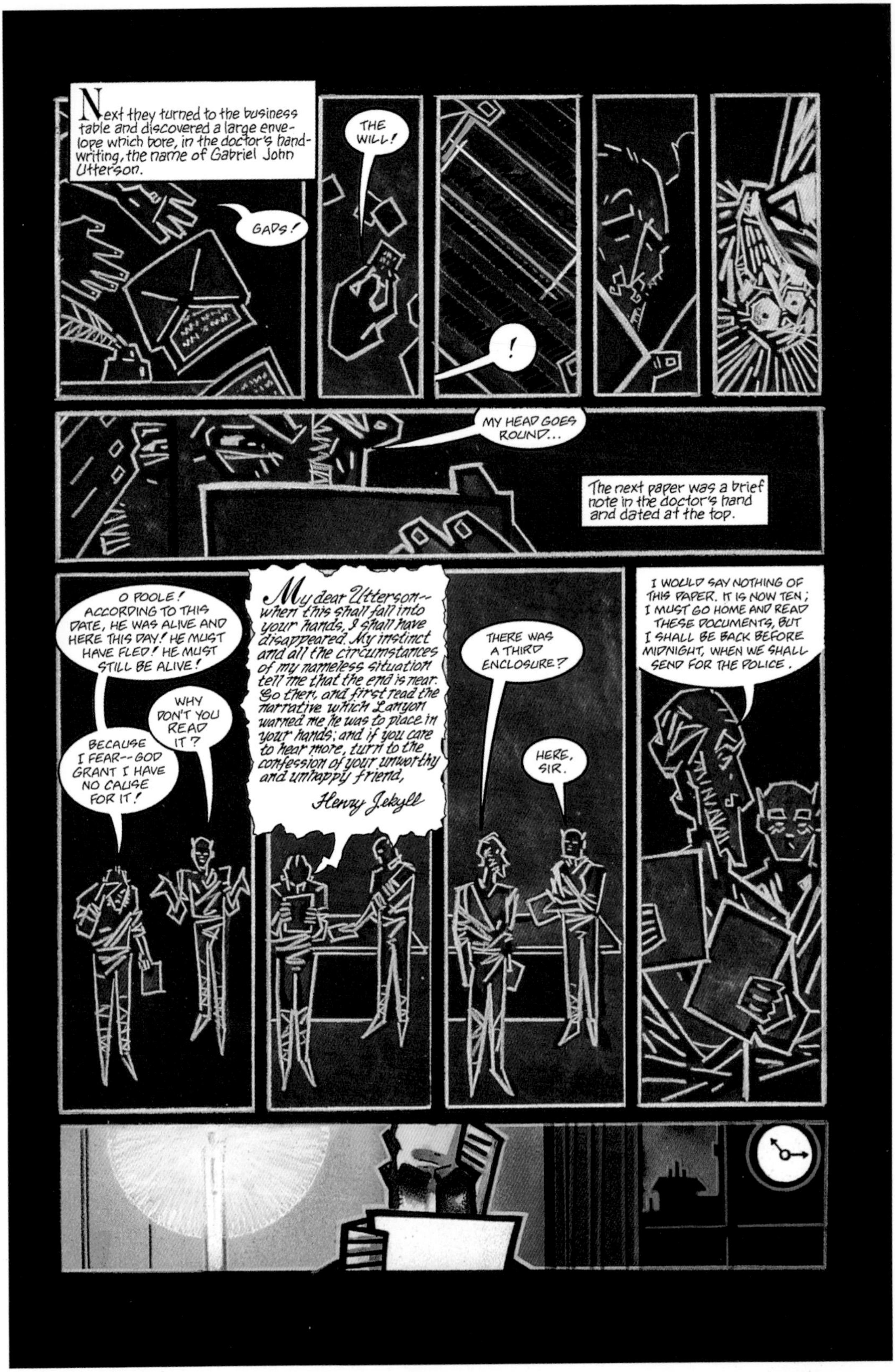
Next they turned to the business table and discovered a large envelope which bore, in the doctor's handwriting, the name of Gabriel John Utterson.
GADS!
THE WILL!
!
MY HEAD GOES ROUND...
The next paper was a brief note in the doctor's hand and dated at the top.
O POOLE! ACCORDING TO THIS DATE, HE WAS ALIVE AND HERE THIS DAY! HE MUST HAVE FLED! HE MUST STILL BE ALIVE!
WHY DON'T YOU READ IT?
BECAUSE I FEAR--GOD GRANT I HAVE NO CAUSE FOR IT!
My dear Utterson-- when this shall fall into your hands, I shall have disappeared. My instinct and all the circumstances of my nameless situation tell me that the end is near. Go then, and first read the narrative which Lanyon warned me he was to place in your hands; and if you care to hear more, turn to the confession of your unworthy and unhappy friend,
Henry Jekyll
THERE WAS A THIRD ENCLOSURE?
HERE, SIR.
I WOULD SAY NOTHING OF THIS PAPER. IT IS NOW TEN; I MUST GO HOME AND READ THESE DOCUMENTS, BUT I SHALL BE BACK BEFORE MIDNIGHT, WHEN WE SHALL SEND FOR THE POLICE.

DR. LANYON'S NARRATIVE

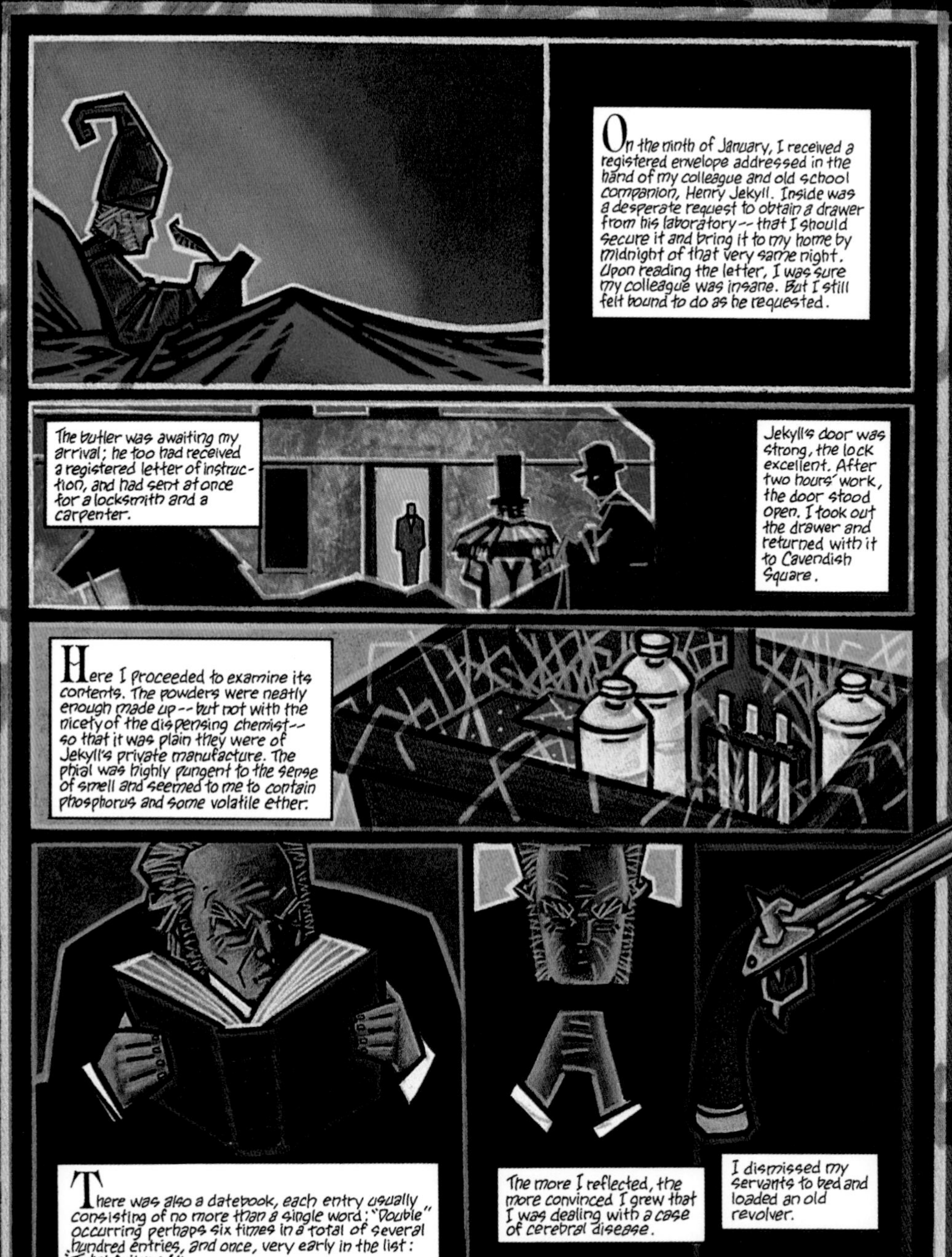

On the ninth of January, I received a registered envelope addressed in the hand of my colleague and old school companion, Henry Jekyll. Inside was a desperate request to obtain a drawer from his laboratory -- that I should secure it and bring it to my home by midnight of that very same night. Upon reading the letter, I was sure my colleague was insane. But I still felt bound to do as he requested.
The butler was awaiting my arrival; he too had received a registered letter of instruction, and had sent at once for a locksmith and a carpenter.
Jekyll's door was strong, the lock excellent. After two hours' work, the door stood open. I took out the drawer and returned with it to Cavendish Square.
Here I proceeded to examine its contents. The powders were neatly enough made up -- but not with the nicety of the dispensing chemist -- so that it was plain they were of Jekyll's private manufacture. The phial was highly pungent to the sense of smell and seemed to me to contain phosphorus and some volatile ether.
There was also a datebook, each entry usually consisting of no more than a single word: "Double" occurring perhaps six times in a total of several hundred entries, and once, very early in the list: "Total failure!"
The more I reflected, the more convinced I grew that I was dealing with a case of cerebral disease.
I dismissed my servants to bed and loaded an old revolver.

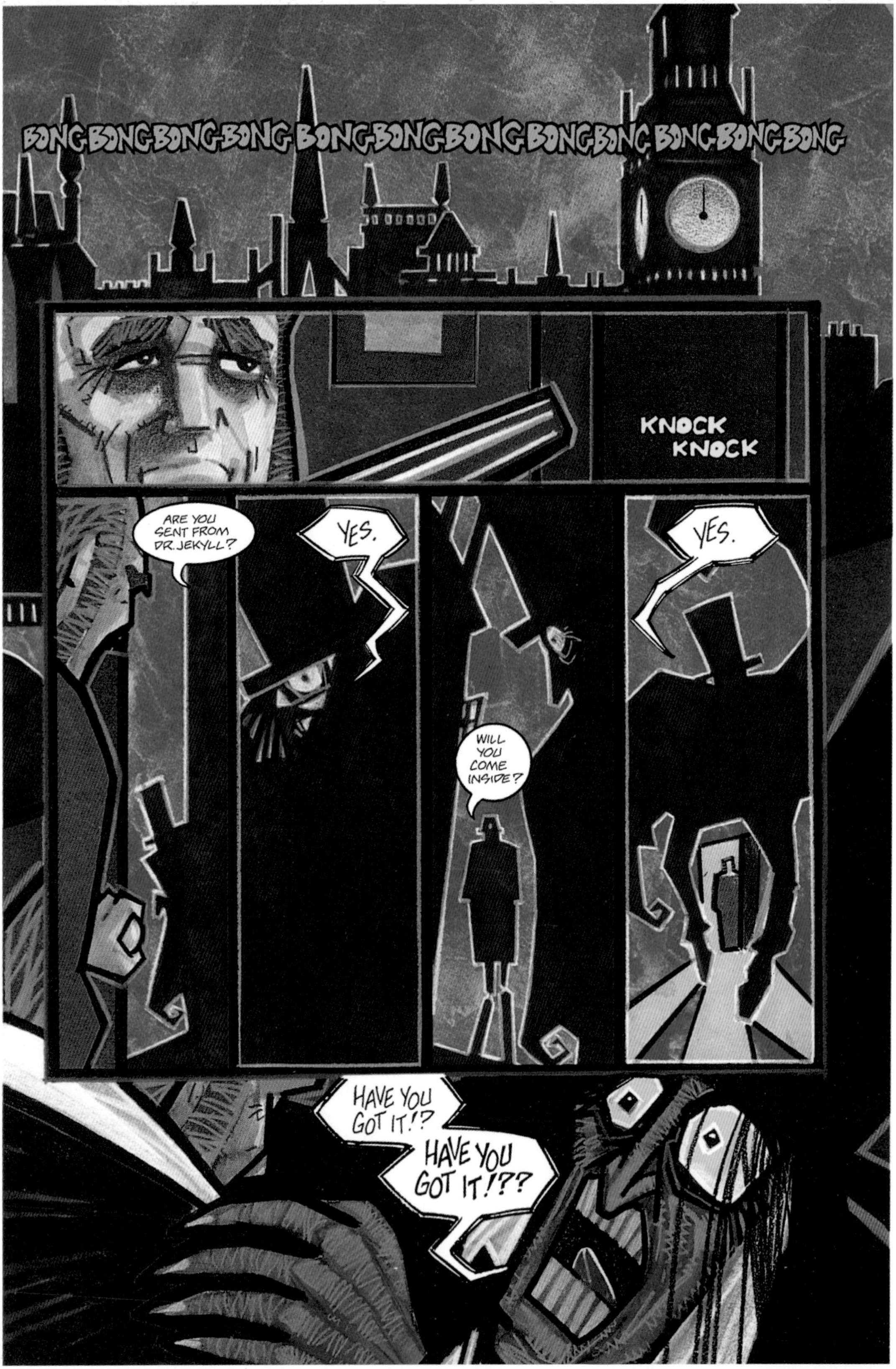
BONG BONG BONG BONG BONG BONG BONG BONG BONG BONG BONG BONG
KNOCK KNOCK
ARE YOU SENT FROM DR. JEKYLL?
YES.
WILL YOU COME INSIDE?
YES.
HAVE YOU GOT IT!?
HAVE YOU GOT IT!??

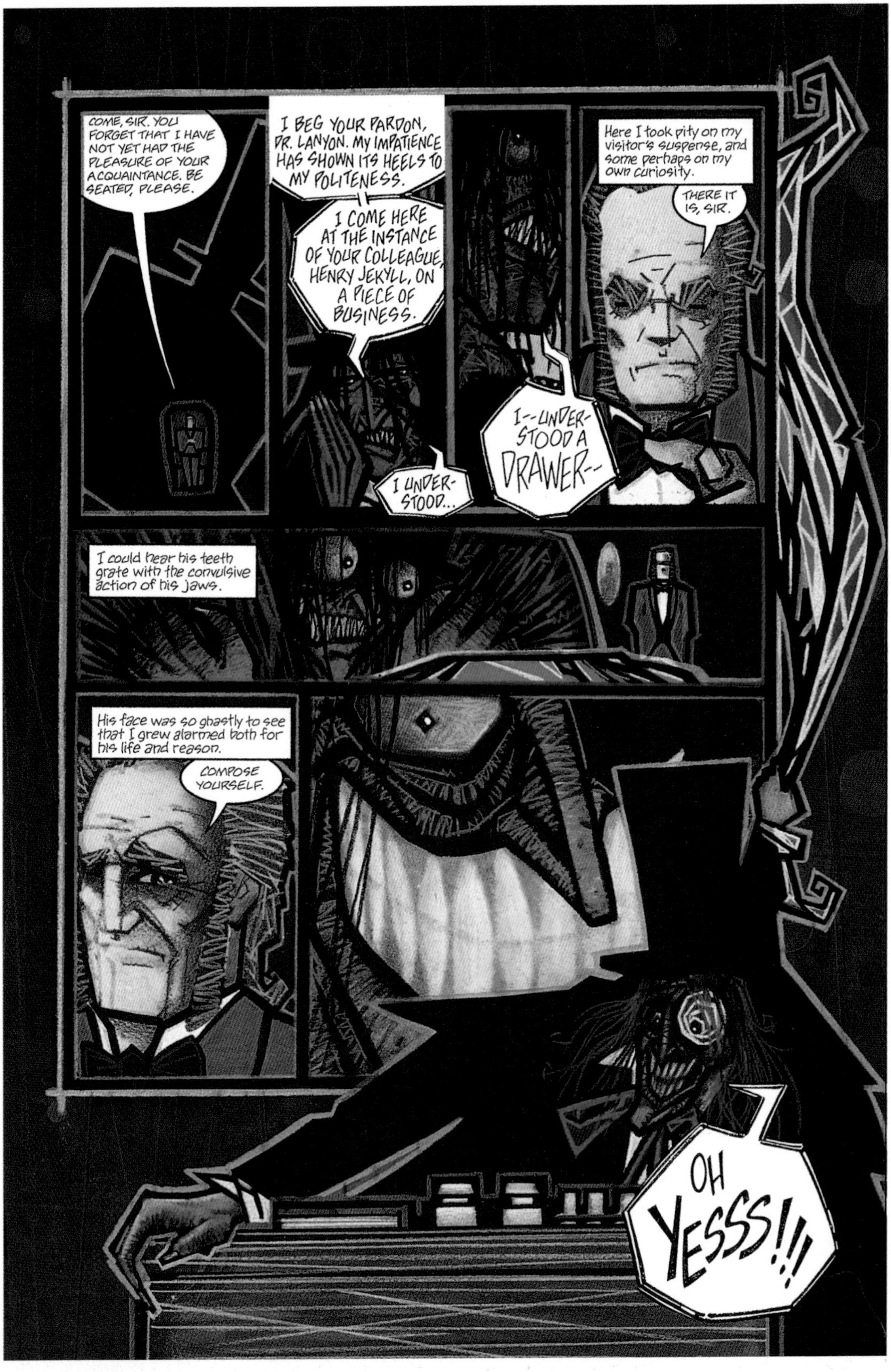
COME, SIR. YOU FORGET THAT I HAVE NOT YET HAD THE PLEASURE OF YOUR ACQUAINTANCE. BE SEATED, PLEASE.
I BEG YOUR PARDON, DR. LANYON. MY IMPATIENCE HAS SHOWN ITS HEELS TO MY POLITENESS.
I COME HERE AT THE INSTANCE OF YOUR COLLEAGUE, HENRY JEKYLL, ON A PIECE OF BUSINESS.
I UNDER-STOOD...
I--UNDER-STOOD A DRAWER--
Here I took pity on my visitor's suspense, and some perhaps on my own curiosity.
THERE IT IS, SIR.
I could hear his teeth grate with the convulsive action of his jaws.
His face was so ghastly to see that I grew alarmed both for his life and reason.
COMPOSE YOURSELF.
OH YESSS!!!

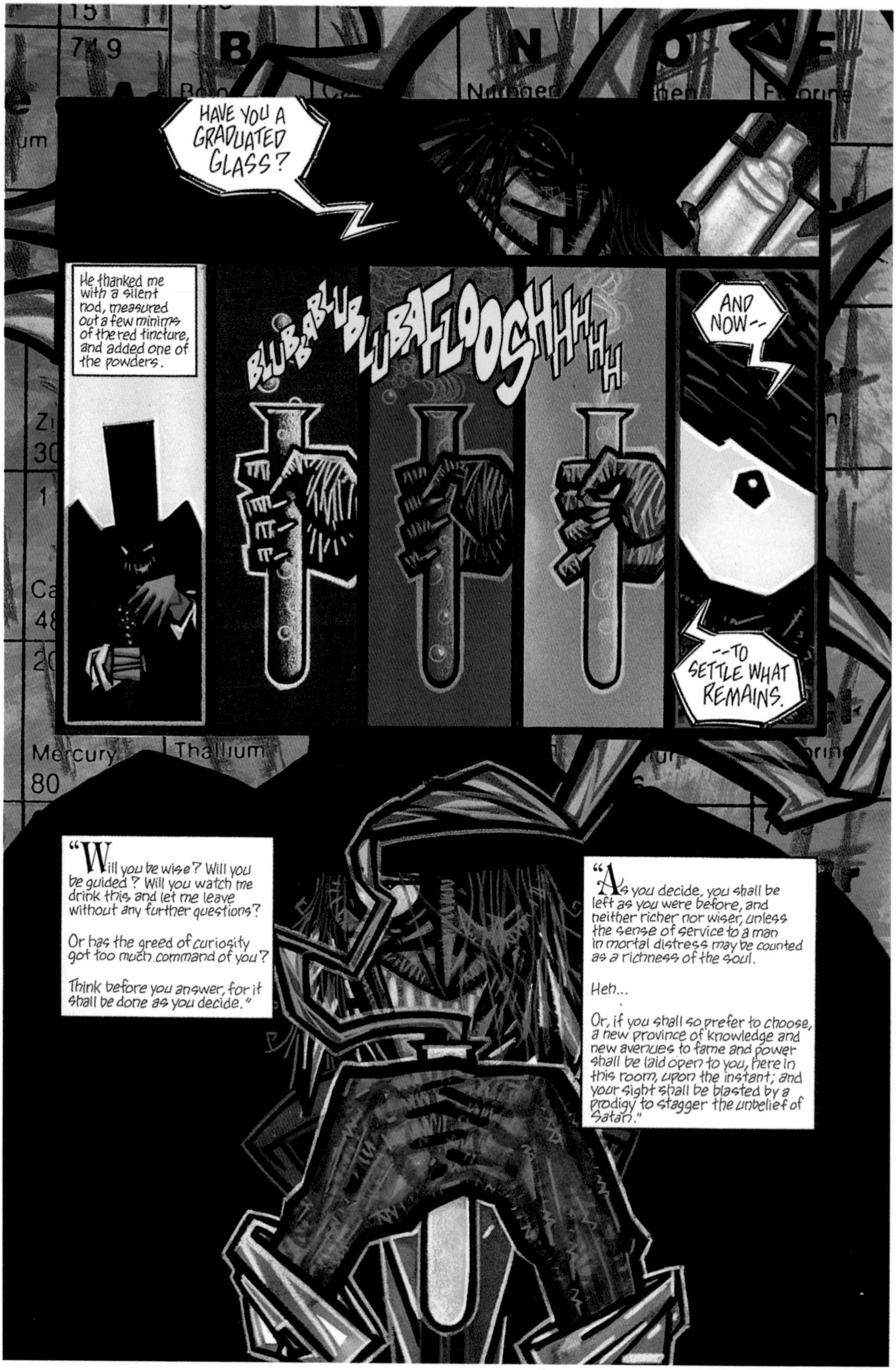
HAVE YOU A GRADUATED GLASS?
He thanked me with a silent nod, measured out a few minims of the red tincture, and added one of the powders.
BLUBBABLUB BLUBAFLOOSHHHHHH
AND NOW--
--TO SETTLE WHAT REMAINS.
"Will you be wise? Will you be guided? Will you watch me drink this and let me leave without any further questions?
Or has the greed of curiosity got too much command of you?
Think before you answer, for it shall be done as you decide."
"As you decide, you shall be left as you were before, and neither richer nor wiser, unless the sense of service to a man in mortal distress may be counted as a richness of the soul.
Heh...
Or, if you shall so prefer to choose, a new province of knowledge and new avenues to fame and power shall be laid open to you, here in this room, upon the instant; and your sight shall be blasted by a prodigy to stagger the unbelief of Satan."

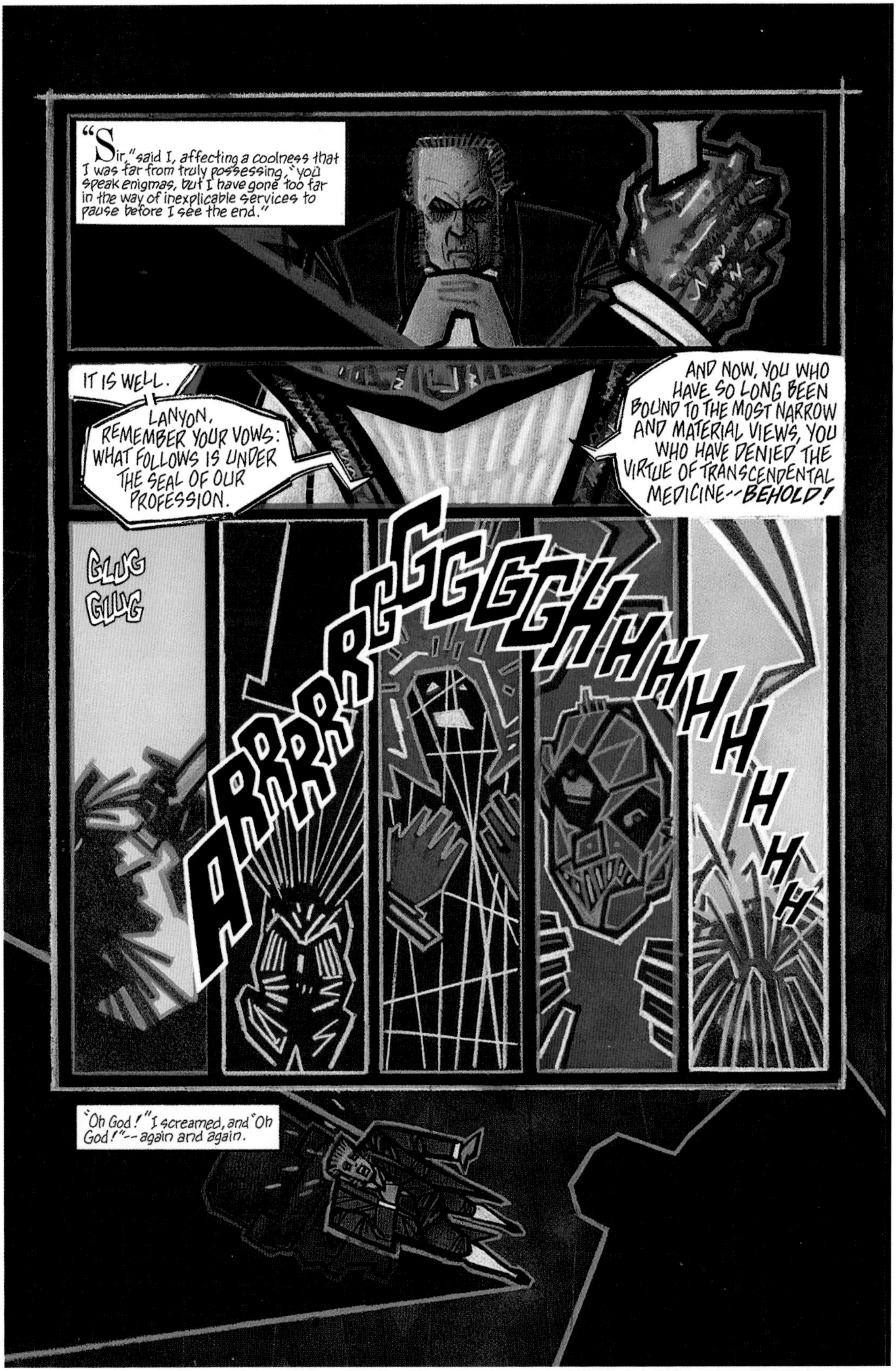
"Sir," said I, affecting a coolness that I was far from truly possessing, "you speak enigmas, but I have gone too far in the way of inexplicable services to pause before I see the end."
IT IS WELL.
LANYON, REMEMBER YOUR VOWS: WHAT FOLLOWS IS UNDER THE SEAL OF OUR PROFESSION.
AND NOW, YOU WHO HAVE SO LONG BEEN BOUND TO THE MOST NARROW AND MATERIAL VIEWS, YOU WHO HAVE DENIED THE VIRTUE OF TRANSCENDENTAL MEDICINE--BEHOLD!
GLUG GLUG
ARRRRRGGGGGHHHHHHHHHH
"Oh God!" I screamed, and "Oh God!"-- again and again.

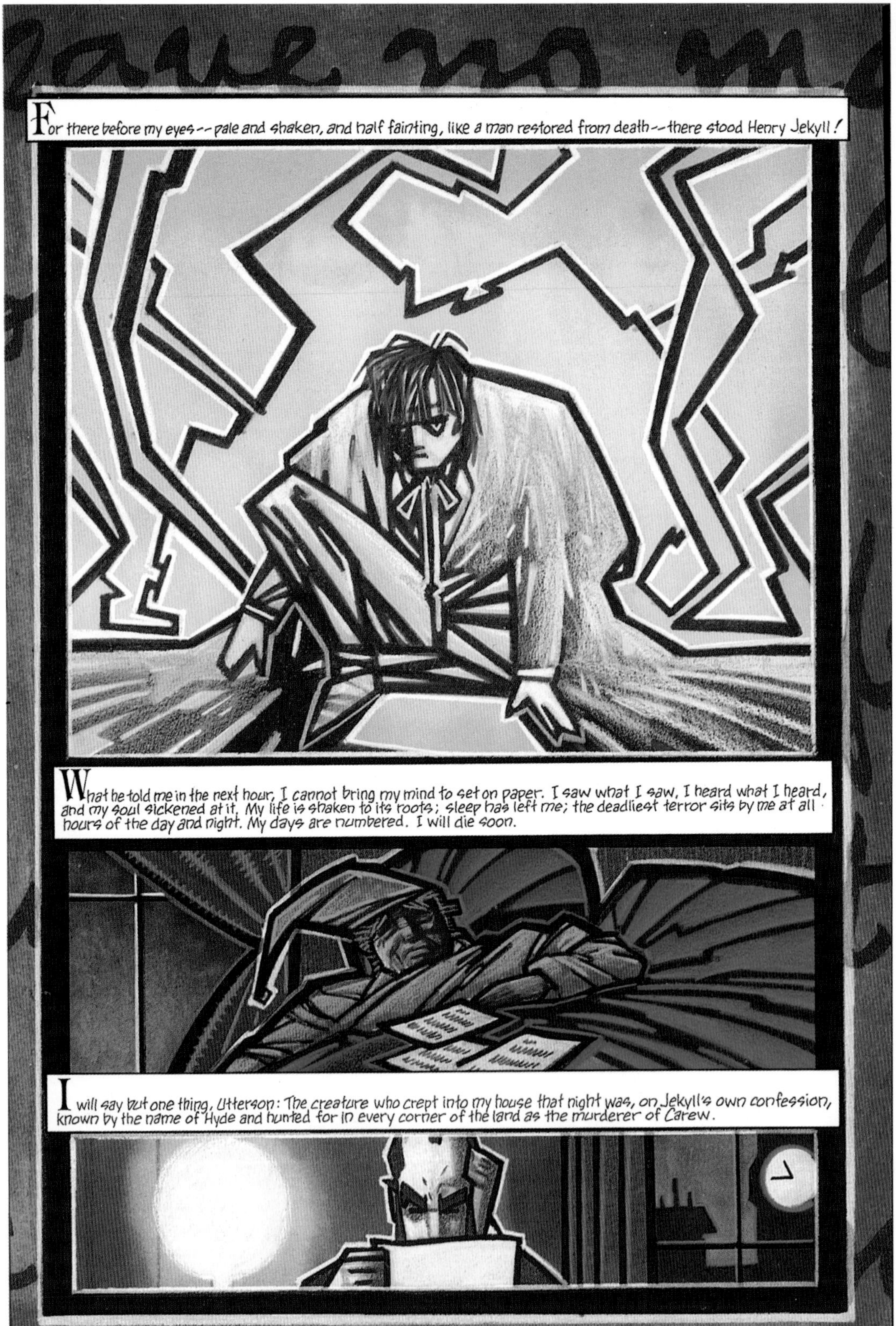
For there before my eyes-- pale and shaken, and half fainting, like a man restored from death-- there stood Henry Jekyll!
What he told me in the next hour, I cannot bring my mind to set on paper. I saw what I saw, I heard what I heard, and my soul sickened at it. My life is shaken to its roots; sleep has left me; the deadliest terror sits by me at all hours of the day and night. My days are numbered. I will die soon.
I will say but one thing, Utterson: The creature who crept into my house that night was, on Jekyll's own confession, known by the name of Hyde and hunted for in every corner of the land as the murderer of Carew.

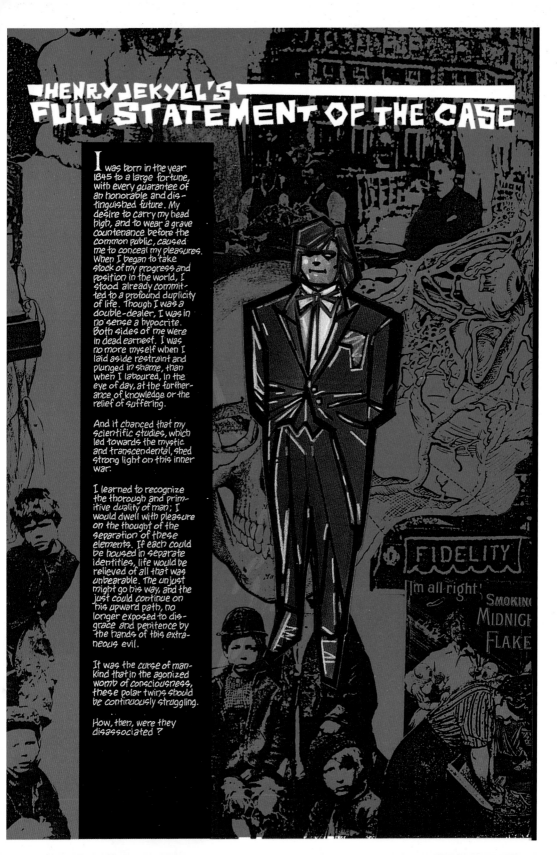

HENRY JEKYLL'S FULL STATEMENT OF THE CASE

I was born in the year 1845 to a large fortune, with every guarantee of an honorable and distinguished future. My desire to carry my head high, and to wear a grave countenance before the common public, caused me to conceal my pleasures. When I began to take stock of my progress and position in the world, I stood already committed to a profound duplicity of life. Though I was a double-dealer, I was in no sense a hypocrite. Both sides of me were in dead earnest. I was no more myself when I laid aside restraint and plunged in shame, than when I laboured, in the eye of day, at the furtherance of knowledge or the relief of suffering.

And it chanced that my scientific studies, which led towards the mystic and transcendental, shed strong light on this inner war.

I learned to recognize the thorough and primitive duality of man; I would dwell with pleasure on the thought of the separation of these elements. If each could be housed in separate identities, life would be relieved of all that was unbearable. The unjust might go his way, and the just could continue on his upward path, no longer exposed to disgrace and penitence by the hands of this extraneous evil.

It was the curse of mankind that in the agonized womb of consciousness, these polar twins should be continuously struggling.

How, then, were they disassociated ?

FIDELITY
I'm all right!
SMOKIN
MIDNIGH
FLAKE

Certain agents, I have discovered, have the power to shake and pluck back that fleshy vestment. For two good reasons, I will not enter deeply into this scientific branch of my confession. First, because I have been made to learn that the doom of our life is bound on our shoulders, and when any attempt is made to cast it off, it returns upon us with more unfamiliar and more awful pressure. Second, because, alas! my discoveries were incomplete.

I knew well I risked death; but the temptation of discovery at last overcame the suggestions of alarm.

I had long since prepared my tincture; I immediately purchased from a firm of wholesale chemists a large quantity of a particular salt which was the last ingredient required. Late one accursed night, I compounded the elements, and drank the foul mixture.

The most racking pangs succeeded: a grinding in the bones, deadly nausea, and a horror of the spirit that cannot be exceeded at the hour of birth or death. Then, there was something indescribably new and, from its very novelty, incredibly sweet.

I felt younger, lighter, happier in body -- a solution of the bonds of obligation, an unknown but not an innocent freedom of the soul. Searching for a mirror, I stole through the corridors, a stranger in my own house. Coming to my room, I saw for the first time the appearance of Edward Hyde.

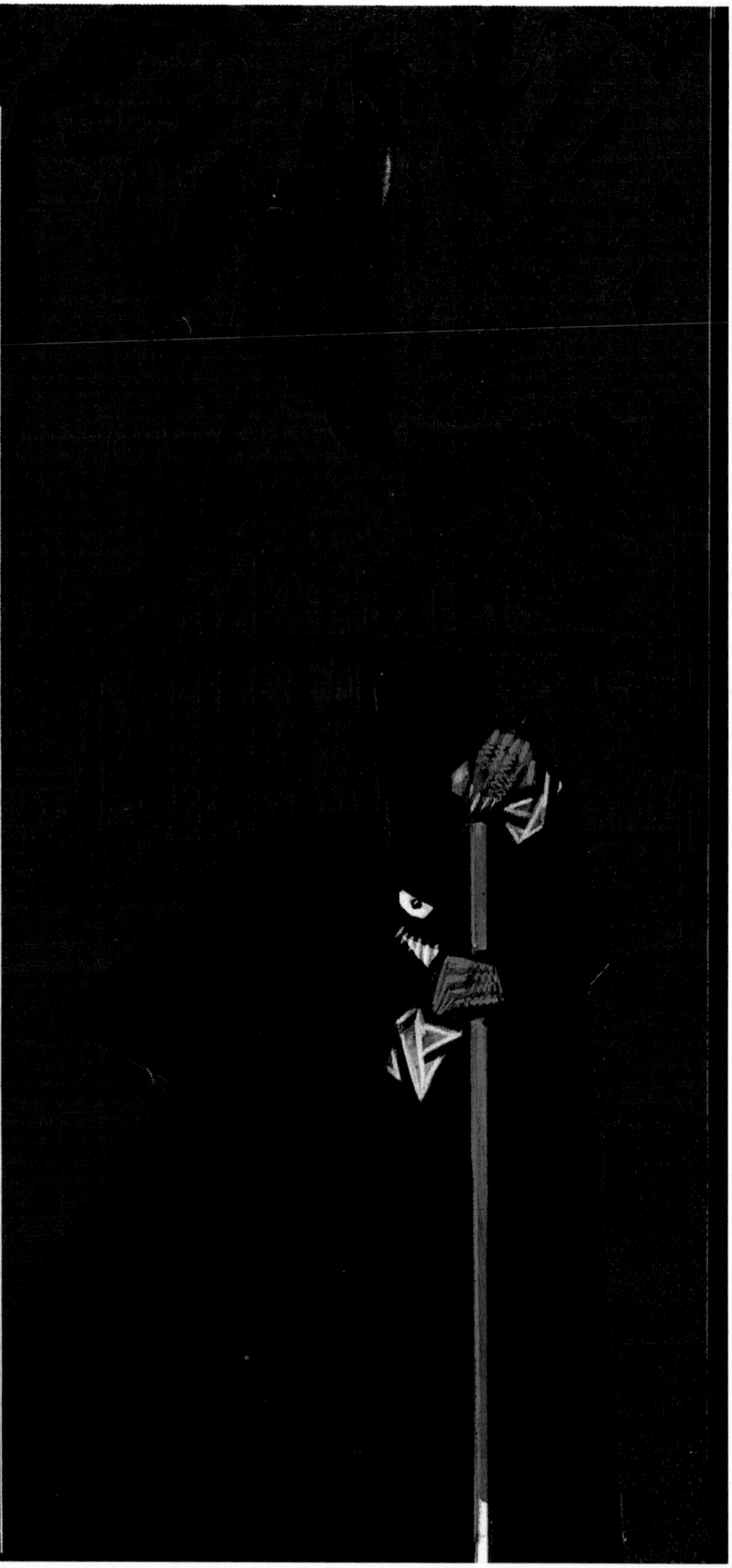

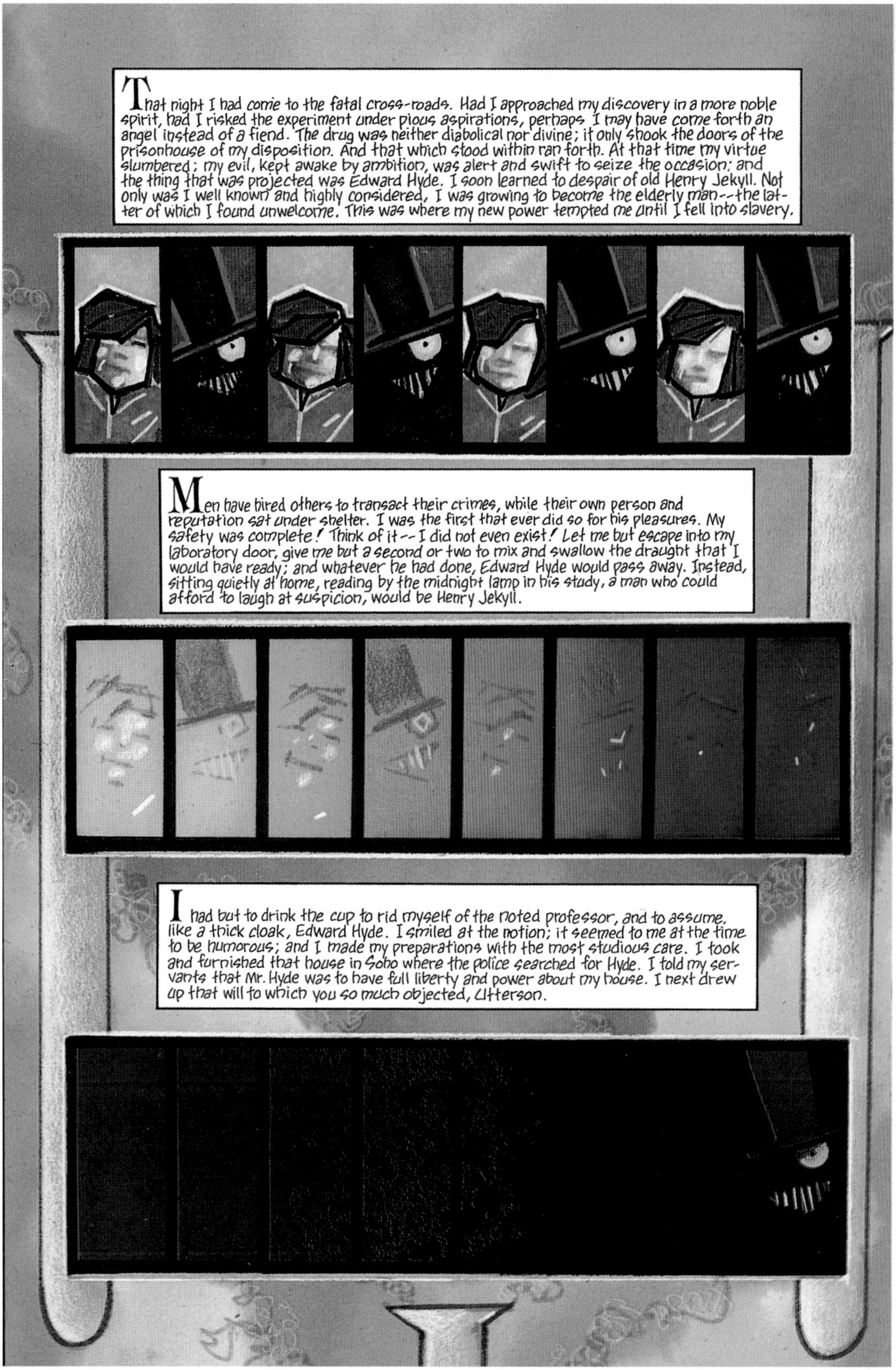

That night I had come to the fatal cross-roads. Had I approached my discovery in a more noble spirit, had I risked the experiment under pious aspirations, perhaps I may have come forth an angel instead of a fiend. The drug was neither diabolical nor divine; it only shook the doors of the prisonhouse of my disposition. And that which stood within ran forth. At that time my virtue slumbered; my evil, kept awake by ambition, was alert and swift to seize the occasion; and the thing that was projected was Edward Hyde. I soon learned to despair of old Henry Jekyll. Not only was I well known and highly considered, I was growing to become the elderly man—the latter of which I found unwelcome. This was where my new power tempted me until I fell into slavery.

Men have hired others to transact their crimes, while their own person and reputation sat under shelter. I was the first that ever did so for his pleasures. My safety was complete! Think of it—I did not even exist! Let me but escape into my laboratory door, give me but a second or two to mix and swallow the draught that I would have ready; and whatever he had done, Edward Hyde would pass away. Instead, sitting quietly at home, reading by the midnight lamp in his study, a man who could afford to laugh at suspicion, would be Henry Jekyll.

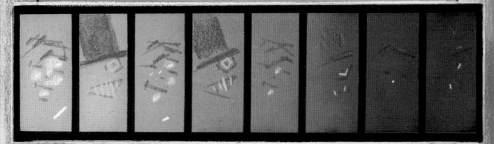

I had but to drink the cup to rid myself of the noted professor, and to assume, like a thick cloak, Edward Hyde. I smiled at the notion; it seemed to me at the time to be humorous; and I made my preparations with the most studious care. I took and furnished that house in Soho where the police searched for Hyde. I told my servants that Mr. Hyde was to have full liberty and power about my house. I next drew up that will to which you so much objected, Utterson.

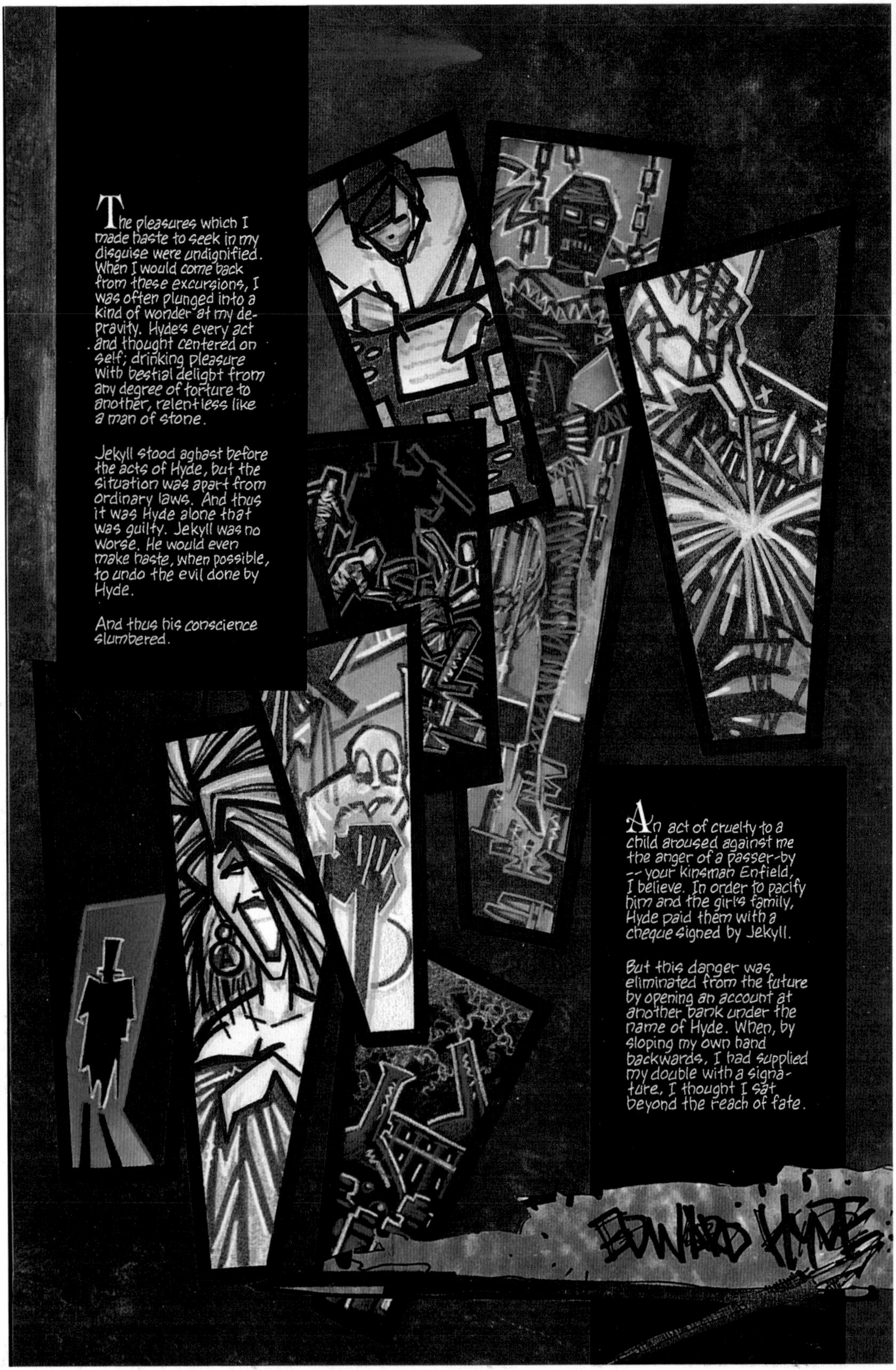
The pleasures which I made haste to seek in my disguise were undignified. When I would come back from these excursions, I was often plunged into a kind of wonder at my depravity. Hyde's every act and thought centered on self; drinking pleasure with bestial delight from any degree of torture to another, relentless like a man of stone.
Jekyll stood aghast before the acts of Hyde, but the situation was apart from ordinary laws. And thus it was Hyde alone that was guilty. Jekyll was no worse. He would even make haste, when possible, to undo the evil done by Hyde.
And thus his conscience slumbered.
An act of cruelty to a child aroused against me the anger of a passer-by -- your kinsman Enfield, I believe. In order to pacify him and the girl's family, Hyde paid them with a cheque signed by Jekyll.
But this danger was eliminated from the future by opening an account at another bank under the name of Hyde. When, by sloping my own hand backwards, I had supplied my double with a signature, I thought I sat beyond the reach of fate.
EDWARD HYDE

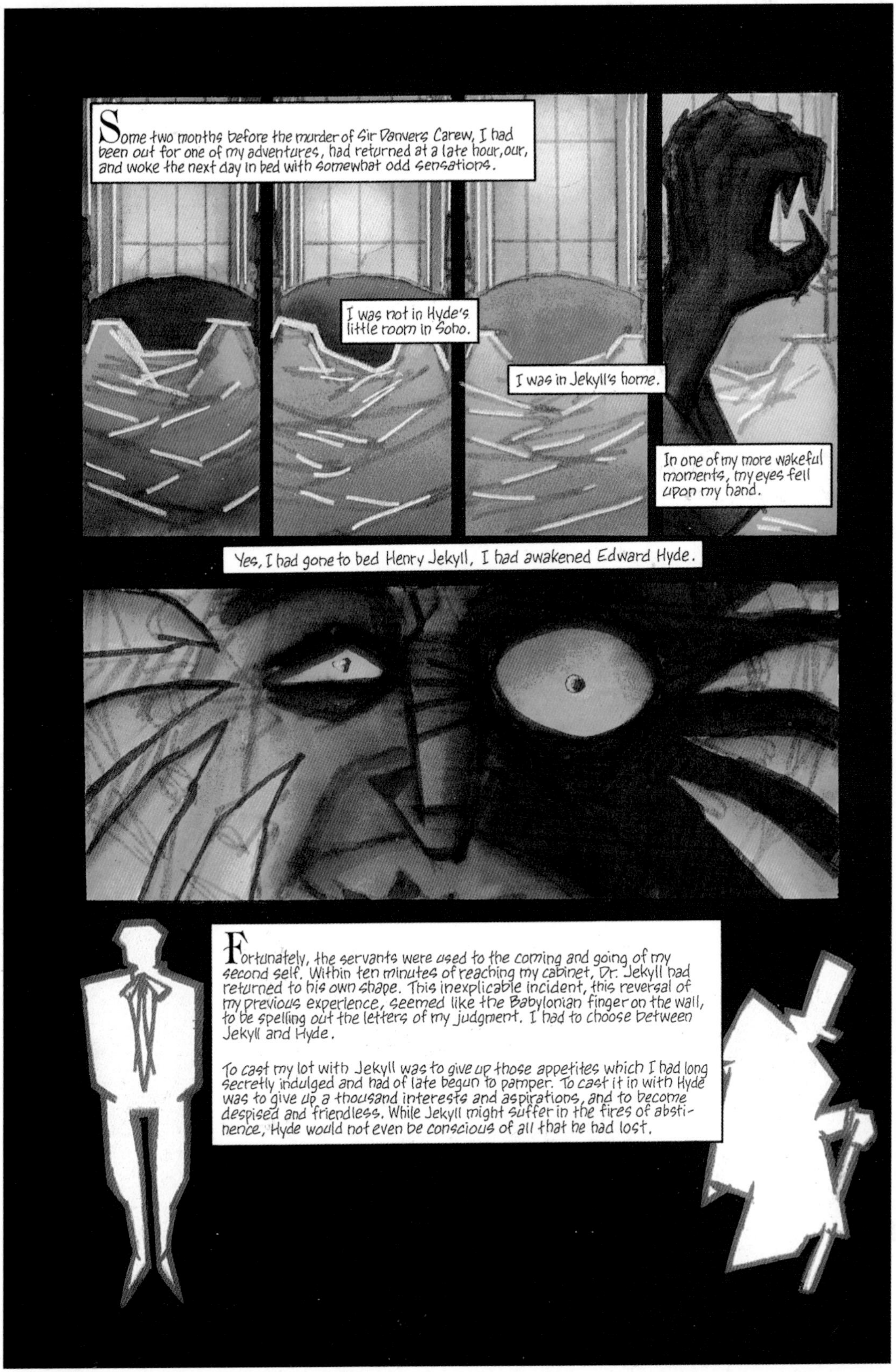
Some two months before the murder of Sir Danvers Carew, I had been out for one of my adventures, had returned at a late hour, our, and woke the next day in bed with somewhat odd sensations.
I was not in Hyde's little room in Soho.
I was in Jekyll's home.
In one of my more wakeful moments, my eyes fell upon my hand.
Yes, I had gone to bed Henry Jekyll, I had awakened Edward Hyde.
Fortunately, the servants were used to the coming and going of my second self. Within ten minutes of reaching my cabinet, Dr. Jekyll had returned to his own shape. This inexplicable incident, this reversal of my previous experience, seemed like the Babylonian finger on the wall, to be spelling out the letters of my judgment. I had to choose between Jekyll and Hyde.
To cast my lot with Jekyll was to give up those appetites which I had long secretly indulged and had of late begun to pamper. To cast it in with Hyde was to give up a thousand interests and aspirations, and to become despised and friendless. While Jekyll might suffer in the fires of abstinence, Hyde would not even be conscious of all that he had lost.

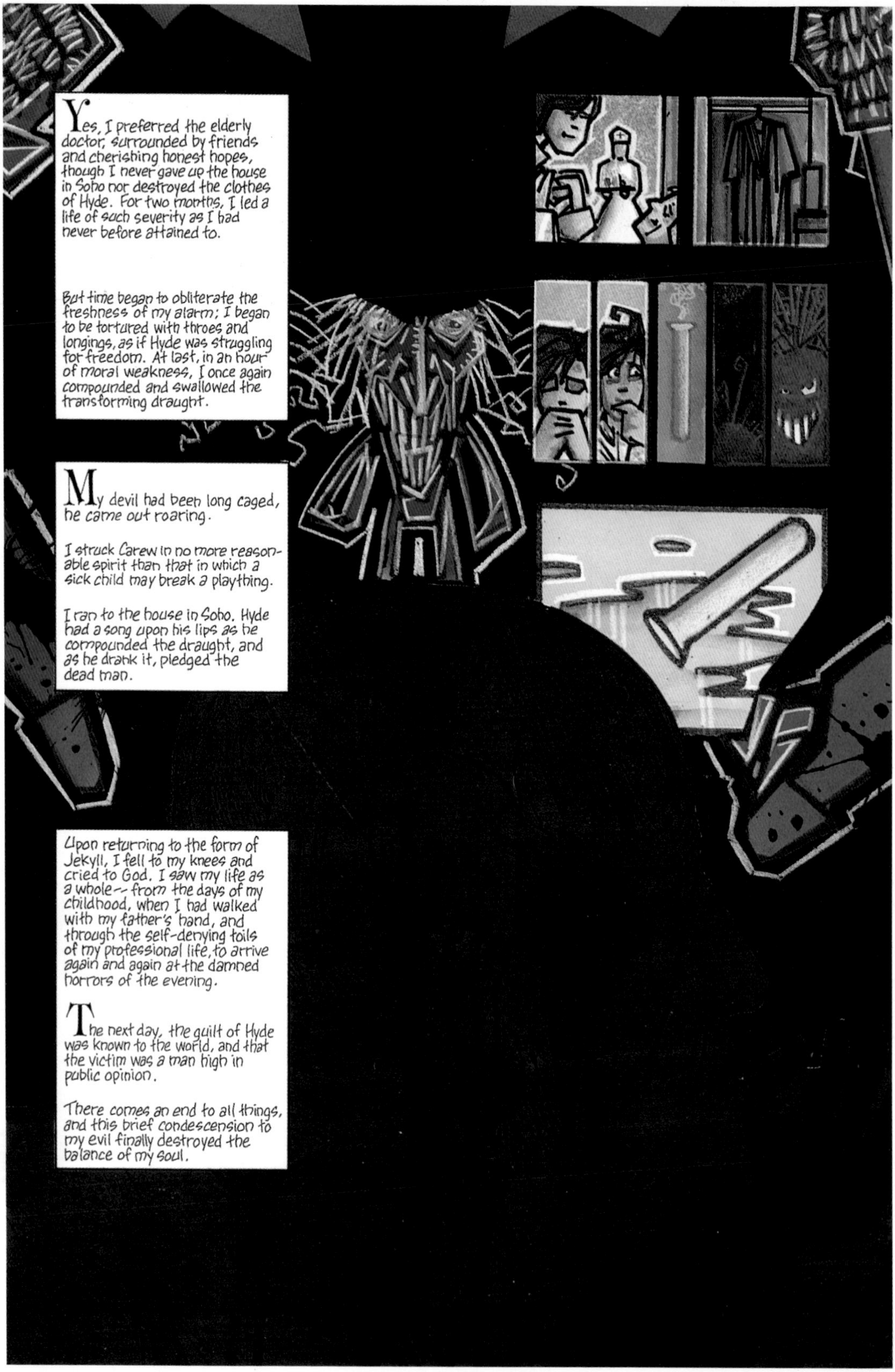
Yes, I preferred the elderly doctor, surrounded by friends and cherishing honest hopes, though I never gave up the house in Soho nor destroyed the clothes of Hyde. For two months, I led a life of such severity as I had never before attained to.
But time began to obliterate the freshness of my alarm; I began to be tortured with throes and longings, as if Hyde was struggling for freedom. At last, in an hour of moral weakness, I once again compounded and swallowed the transforming draught.
My devil had been long caged, he came out roaring.
I struck Carew in no more reasonable spirit than that in which a sick child may break a plaything.
I ran to the house in Soho. Hyde had a song upon his lips as he compounded the draught, and as he drank it, pledged the dead man.
Upon returning to the form of Jekyll, I fell to my knees and cried to God. I saw my life as a whole-- from the days of my childhood, when I had walked with my father's hand, and through the self-denying toils of my professional life, to arrive again and again at the damned horrors of the evening.
The next day, the guilt of Hyde was known to the world, and that the victim was a man high in public opinion.
There comes an end to all things, and this brief condescension to my evil finally destroyed the balance of my soul.

Yet I still was not alarmed until one afternoon this past January in Regent's Park.

My reason wavered, but it did not fail me utterly. I have more than once observed that, in my second character, my faculties seemed sharpened to a point. Where Jekyll might have succumbed, Hyde rose to the importance of the moment. My drugs were in one of the presses of my cabinet; how was I to reach them? Hyde was wanted for murder, he could not return to my home.

Hyde in danger of his life was a creature new to me; shaken with inordinate anger, strung to the pitch of murder, lusting to inflict pain. Yet, with a great effort, Hyde composed his letters to Lanyon and Poole and somehow made his way to my former colleague's home. While waiting for the midnight hour, a woman spoke to him, offering, I think, a box of lights.

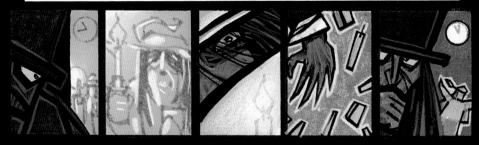

When I came to myself at Lanyon's, the horror of my old friend affected me somewhat: not much, but at least it was a drop in the sea to the abhorrence with which I looked back upon these hours.

A change had come over me. It was no longer the fear of the gallows, it was the horror of being Hyde that racked me.

The morning after my encounter with Lanyon, I was seized again with the indescribable sensations that signaled the change. Soon, I was raging and freezing with the passions of Hyde.

I took on this occasion a double dose to become myself again, and six hours later, the drug had to be readministered.

From that day forth, only under the immediate stimulation of the drug was I able to wear the countenance of Jekyll. If I slept, or even dozed for a moment in my chair, it was always as Hyde that I awakened.

Under the strain of this continually impending doom, I became a creature eaten up and emptied by fever, weak in both body and mind, and solely occupied by one thought: the horror of my other self.

The hatred of Hyde for Jekyll was of a different order. Hyde loathed the despondency into which Jekyll was now fallen, and he resented the dislike with which he was himself regarded. Hence the apelike tricks that he would play me, scrawling in my own hand blasphemies on the pages of my books, burning letters and destroying the portrait of my father. Had it not been for his fear of death, he would have ruined himself in order to ruin me.

But his love of life is wonderful, and I, who sicken and freeze at the mere thought of him, find it in my heart to pity him when I know how he fears my power to cut him off by suicide.

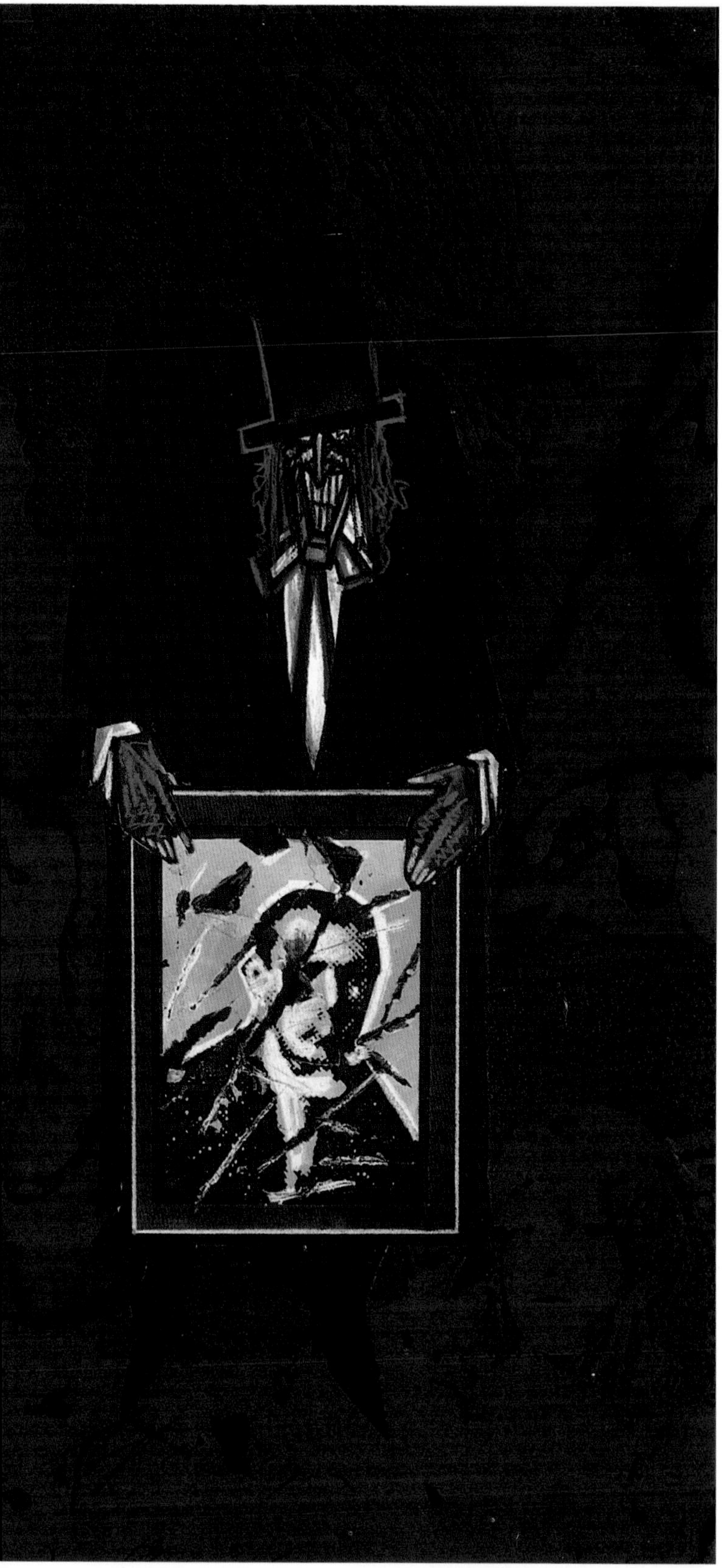

It is useless, and time fails me, to prolong this description. No one has ever suffered such torments -- let that suffice.

My punishment might have gone on for years, but for the last calamity which has now fallen. My provision of the salt, which had never been renewed since the first experiment, began to run low. I sent out for a fresh supply and found it was without efficiency. No doubt Poole has told you how I have had London ransacked in vain.

I now believe that it was my first supply that was impure, and that it was that unknown impurity which affected the draught.

About a week has passed, and I am now finishing this statement under the influence of the old powders. This, then, is the last time Henry Jekyll can think his own thoughts or see his own face (now how sadly altered!). Nor must I delay to bring my writing to an end. Should the throes of change take me in the act of writing it, Hyde will tear it to pieces.

Half an hour from now, when I shall again and forever become that hated personality, will I sit shuddering in my chair, or continue, with the most strained and fearstruck ecstasy of listening, to pace up and down this room (my last earthly refuge) and give ear to every sound of menace?

Will Hyde die upon the gallows?

Or will he find courage to take his life at the last moment?

God knows; I am careless; this is my true hour of death, and what is to follow concerns another than myself.

Here then, I bring the life of that unhappy Dr. Jekyll to an end.

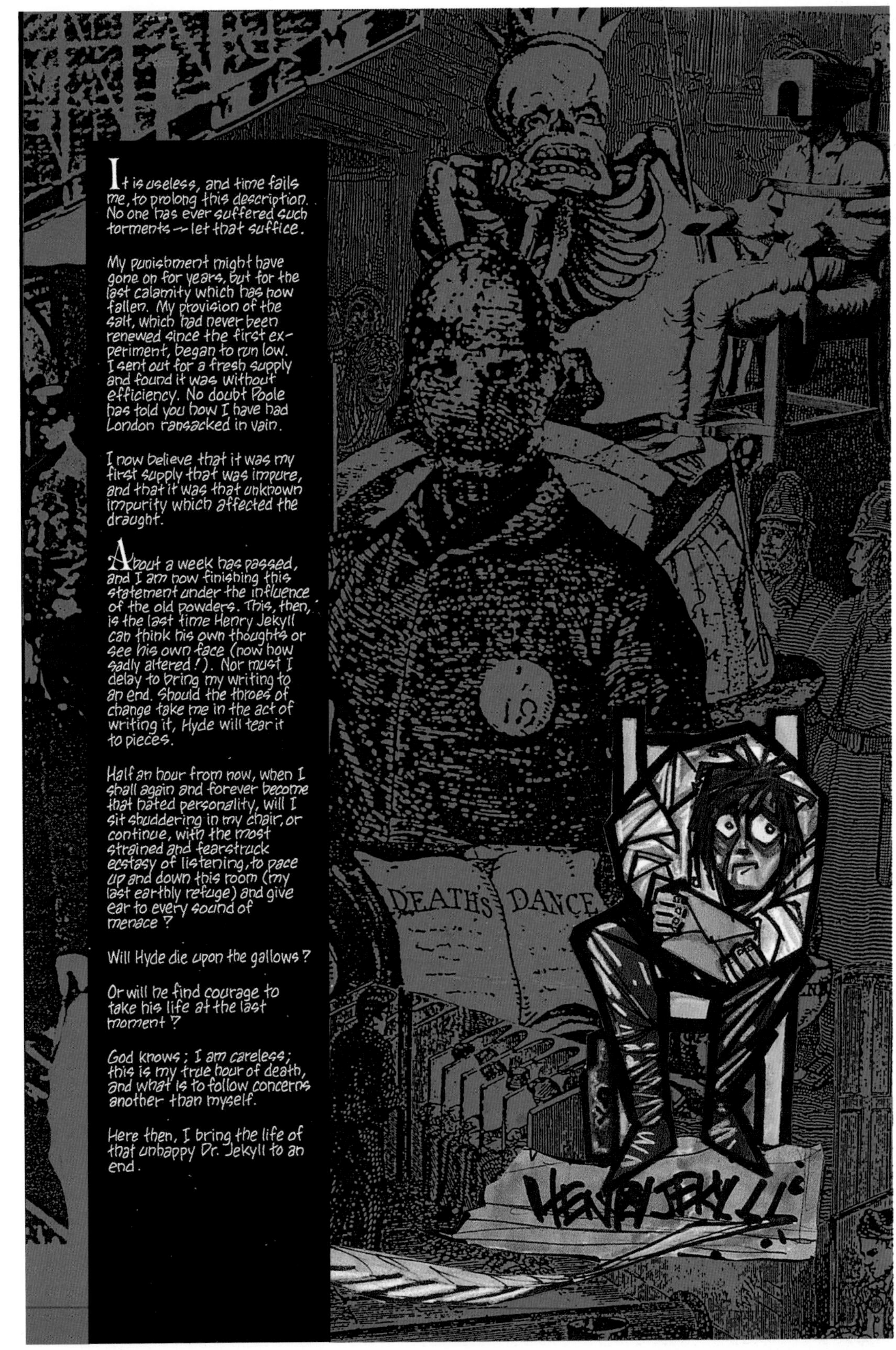
DEATHS DANCE
HENRY JEKYLL

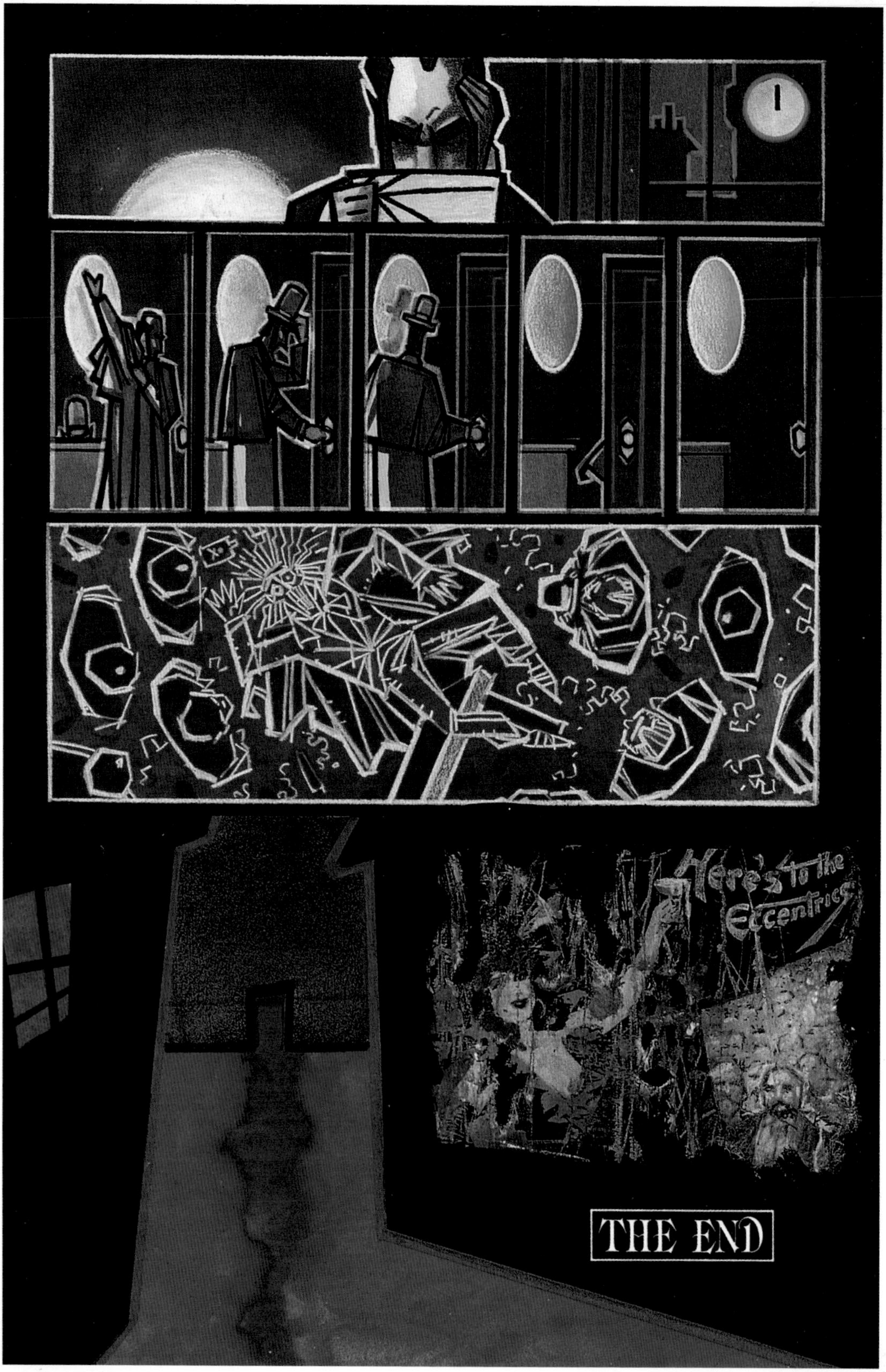
Here's to the Eccentrics
THE END

WATCH OUT FOR PAPERCUTZ™

NOW THAT YOU HAVE READ THE CLASSICS ILLUSTRATED EDITION, DON'T MISS THE ADDED ENJOYMENT OF READING THE ORIGINAL, OBTAINABLE AT YOUR SCHOOL OR PUBLIC LIBRARY.

The above sentence has appeared at the end of many comics adaptations of world-famous novels that have appeared over the years in CLASSICS ILLUSTRATED comicbooks and graphic novels. It's not just a tradition to run that sentence on the story's last page, it's also part of the very spirit of CLASSICS ILLUSTRATED.

And as much as we respect tradition at Papercutz, we didn't add the customary closing sentence to this book's adaptation of Dr. Jekyl and Mr. Hyde simply because it didn't fit in too well with John K. Snyder III's design. That doesn't mean we still don't encourage you to check out Robert Louis Stevenson's brilliant novel—far from it. Our writers and artists try to capture as much of the source material as possible into these short 48-page adaptations, yet there's still so much material that unfortunately must be left out. That's also why we started CLASSICS ILLUSTRATED DELUXE—the companion series to CLASSICS ILLUSTRATED that features much longer adaptations. Check out our preview of Mark Twain's "The Adventures of Tom Sawyer" on the following pages, which will be featured in CLASSICS ILLUSTRATED DELUXE #4. Not only do writers Jean David Morvan and Frederique Voulyzé have 138 pages to adapt Twain's style, it's illustrated by Séverine Lefèbvre in a manga-influenced style!

When CLASSICS ILLUSTRATED was first conceived by Albert Lewis Kanter, it was with the hope of guiding the then-millions of comicbook-reading children to the virtues of "real" literature. Since that time, comics have evolved to the point where it is now accepted as a legitimate art form. Yet comics and graphic novels, like film, are still incredibly compelling to so-called "non-readers," and CLASSICS ILLUSTRATED is still proud to introduce these great works to readers of all ages. But now, we hope our adaptations are written and drawn well enough to stand on their own as works of art. Just as film has adapted works from other media, comics can too, and we hope you like the results!

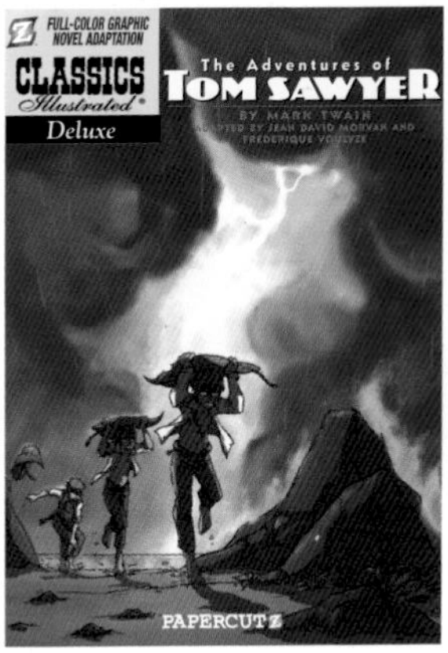
FULL-COLOR GRAPHIC NOVEL ADAPTATION
CLASSICS Illustrated
Deluxe
The Adventures of TOM SAWYER
BY MARK TWAIN
PAPERCUTZ

Thanks,

Jim

Jim Salicrup
PAPERCUTZ
Editor-in-Chief

Special Preview of CLASSICS ILLUSTRATED DELUXE #4
"The Adventures of Tom Sawyer"

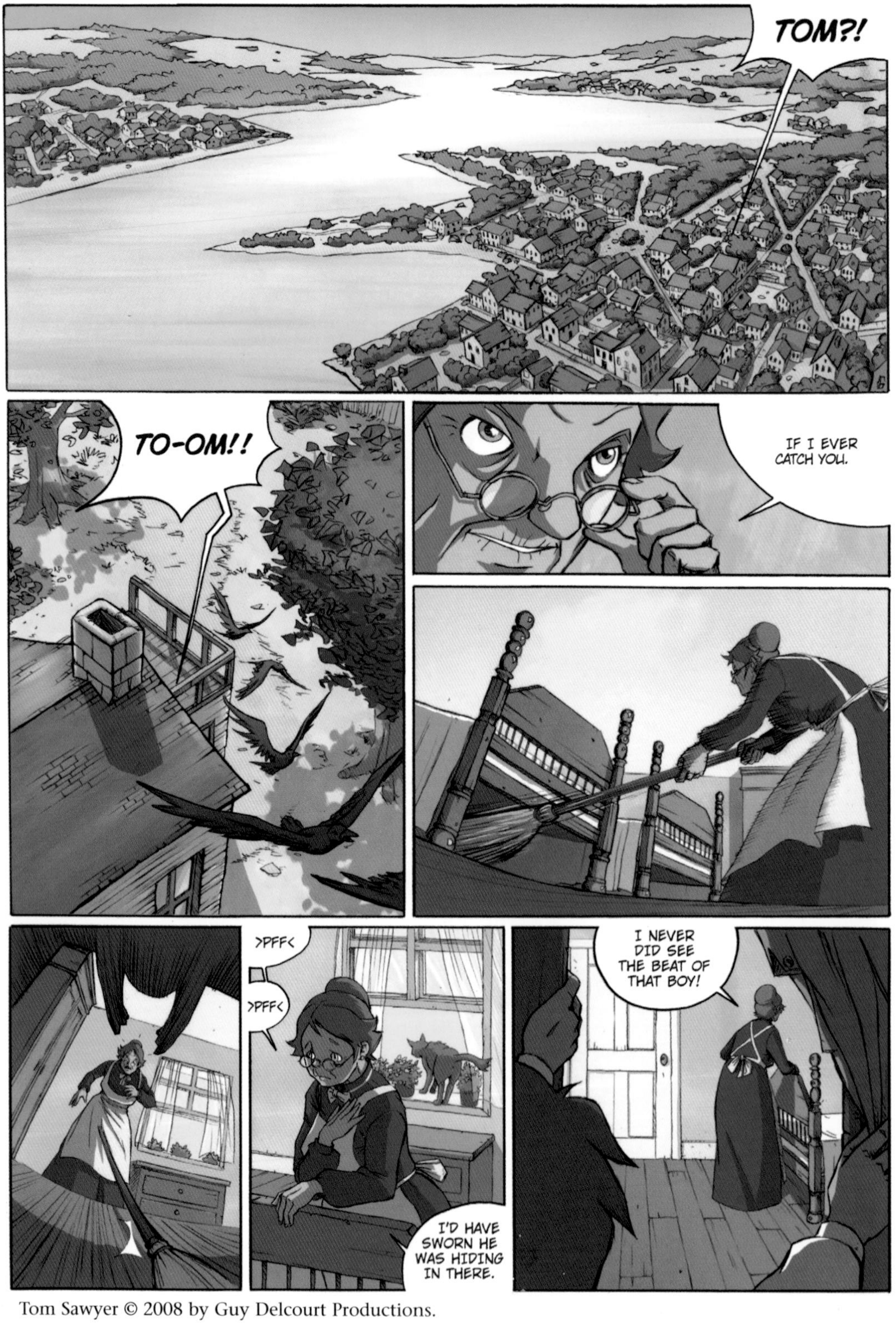
TOM?!
TO-OM!!
IF I EVER CATCH YOU.
>PFF<
>PFF<
I'D HAVE SWORN HE WAS HIDING IN THERE.
I NEVER DID SEE THE BEAT OF THAT BOY!

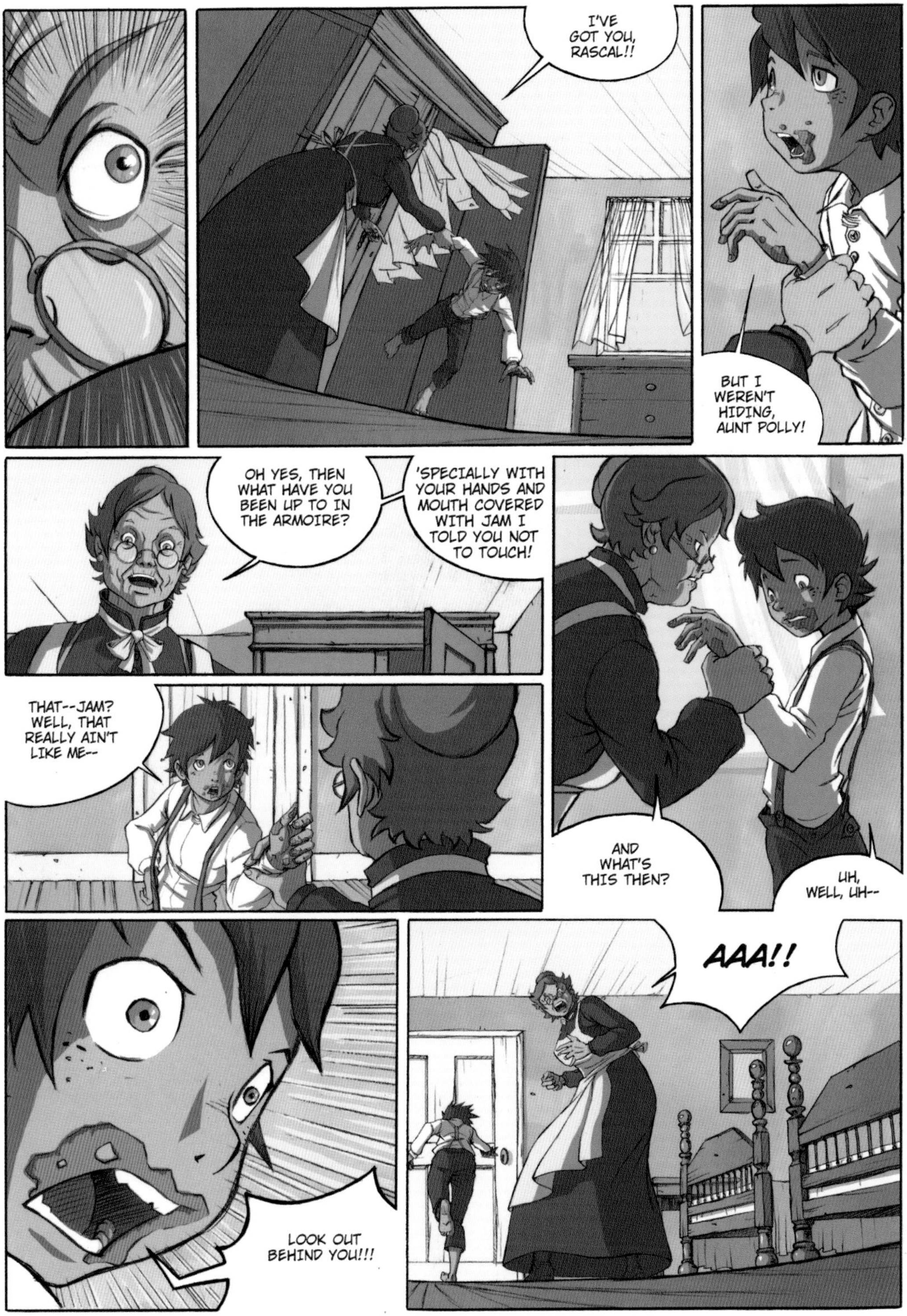
I'VE GOT YOU, RASCAL!!
BUT I WEREN'T HIDING, AUNT POLLY!
OH YES, THEN WHAT HAVE YOU BEEN UP TO IN THE ARMOIRE?
'SPECIALLY WITH YOUR HANDS AND MOUTH COVERED WITH JAM I TOLD YOU NOT TO TOUCH!
THAT--JAM? WELL, THAT REALLY AIN'T LIKE ME--
AND WHAT'S THIS THEN?
UH, WELL, UH--
LOOK OUT BEHIND YOU!!!
AAA!!

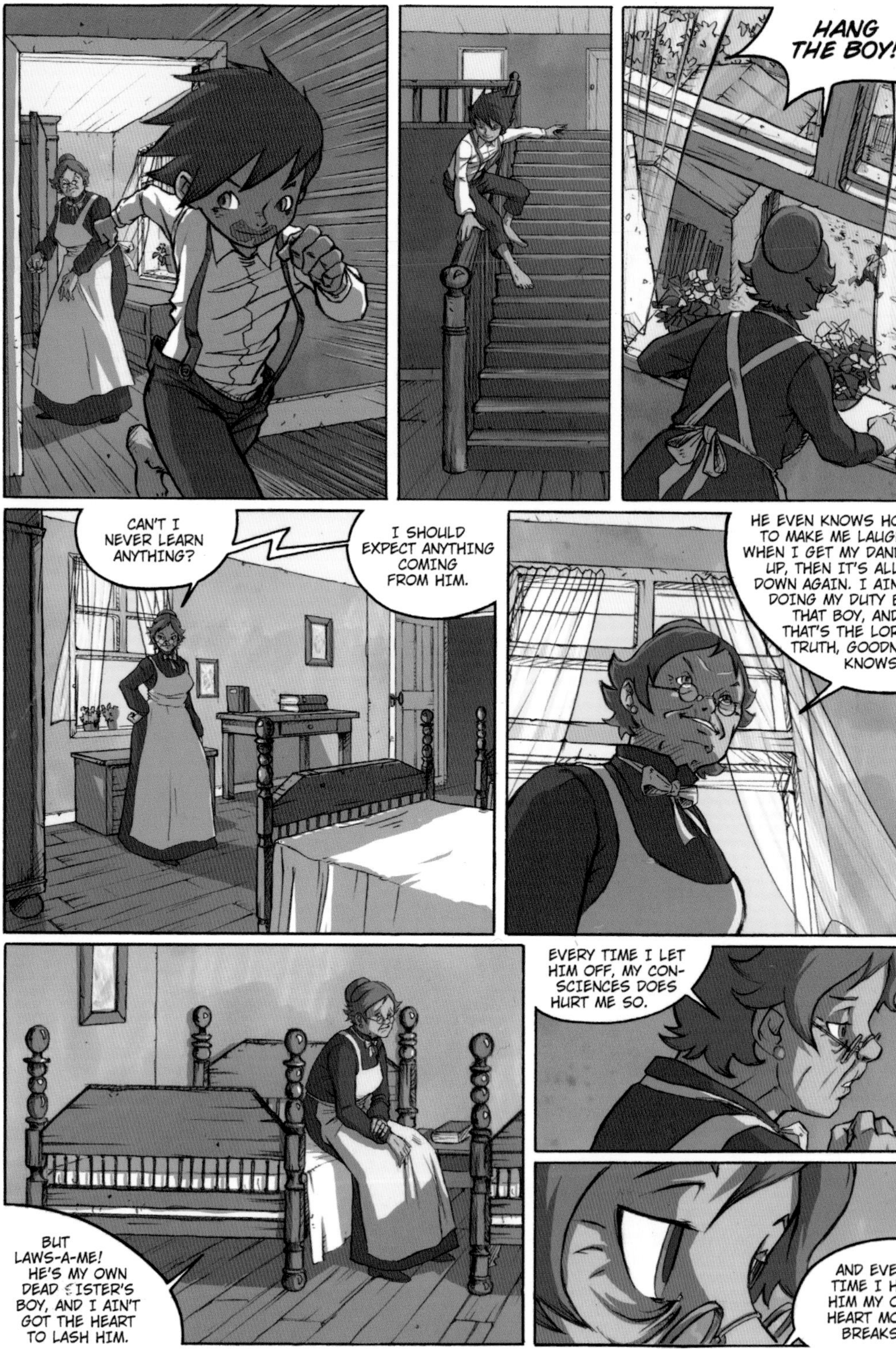

HANG THE BOY!
CAN'T I NEVER LEARN ANYTHING?
I SHOULD EXPECT ANYTHING COMING FROM HIM.
HE EVEN KNOWS HOW TO MAKE ME LAUGH WHEN I GET MY DANDER UP, THEN IT'S ALL DOWN AGAIN. I AIN'T DOING MY DUTY BY THAT BOY, AND THAT'S THE LORD'S TRUTH, GOODNESS KNOWS.
BUT LAWS-A-ME! HE'S MY OWN DEAD SISTER'S BOY, AND I AIN'T GOT THE HEART TO LASH HIM.
EVERY TIME I LET HIM OFF, MY CONSCIENCES DOES HURT ME SO.
AND EVERY TIME I HIT HIM MY OLD HEART MOST BREAKS.

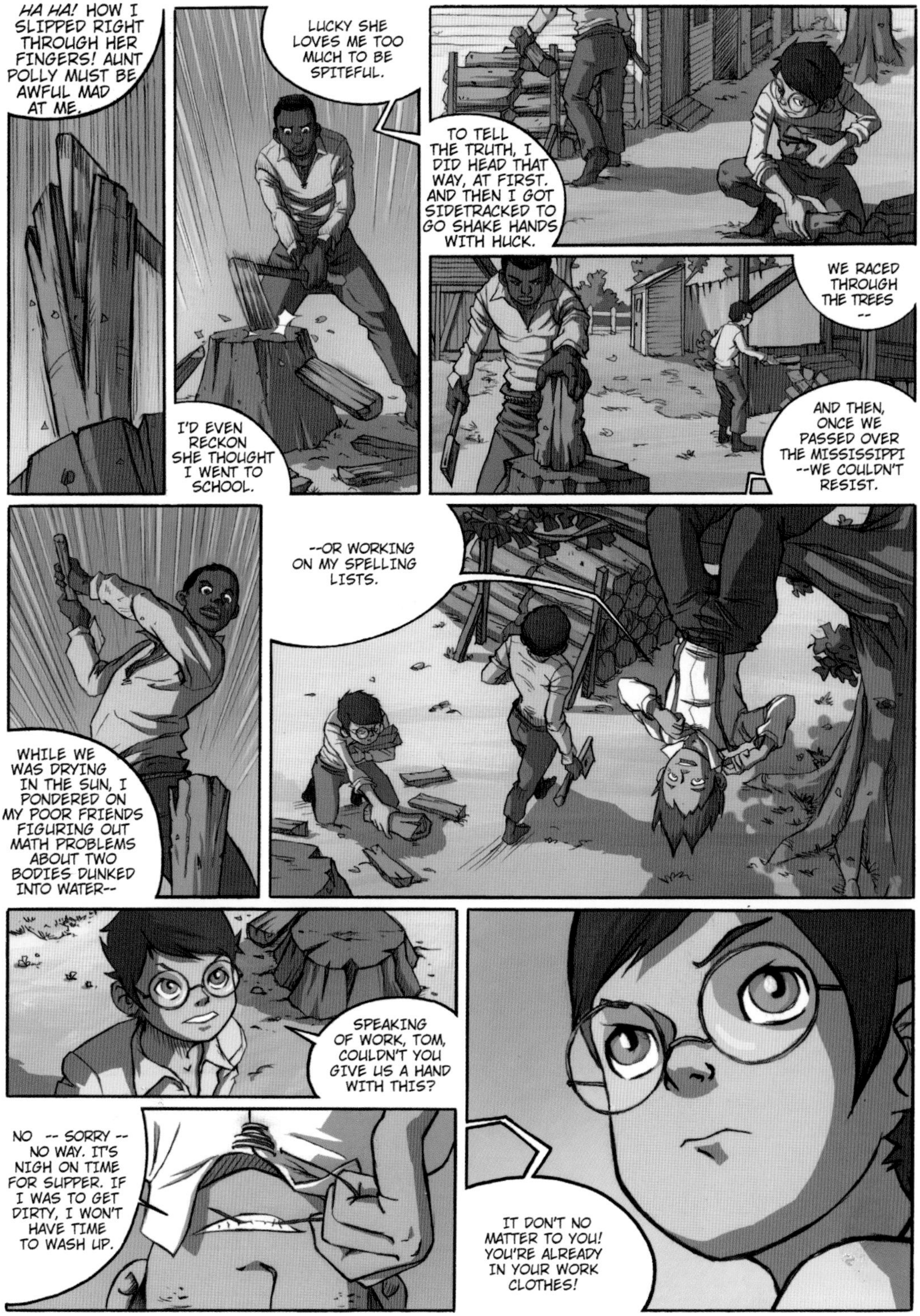
HA HA! HOW I SLIPPED RIGHT THROUGH HER FINGERS! AUNT POLLY MUST BE AWFUL MAD AT ME.
LUCKY SHE LOVES ME TOO MUCH TO BE SPITEFUL.
I'D EVEN RECKON SHE THOUGHT I WENT TO SCHOOL.
TO TELL THE TRUTH, I DID HEAD THAT WAY, AT FIRST. AND THEN I GOT SIDETRACKED TO GO SHAKE HANDS WITH HUCK.
WE RACED THROUGH THE TREES --
AND THEN, ONCE WE PASSED OVER THE MISSISSIPPI --WE COULDN'T RESIST.
WHILE WE WAS DRYING IN THE SUN, I PONDERED ON MY POOR FRIENDS FIGURING OUT MATH PROBLEMS ABOUT TWO BODIES DUNKED INTO WATER--
--OR WORKING ON MY SPELLING LISTS.
SPEAKING OF WORK, TOM, COULDN'T YOU GIVE US A HAND WITH THIS?
NO -- SORRY -- NO WAY. IT'S NIGH ON TIME FOR SUPPER. IF I WAS TO GET DIRTY, I WON'T HAVE TIME TO WASH UP.
IT DON'T NO MATTER TO YOU! YOU'RE ALREADY IN YOUR WORK CLOTHES!

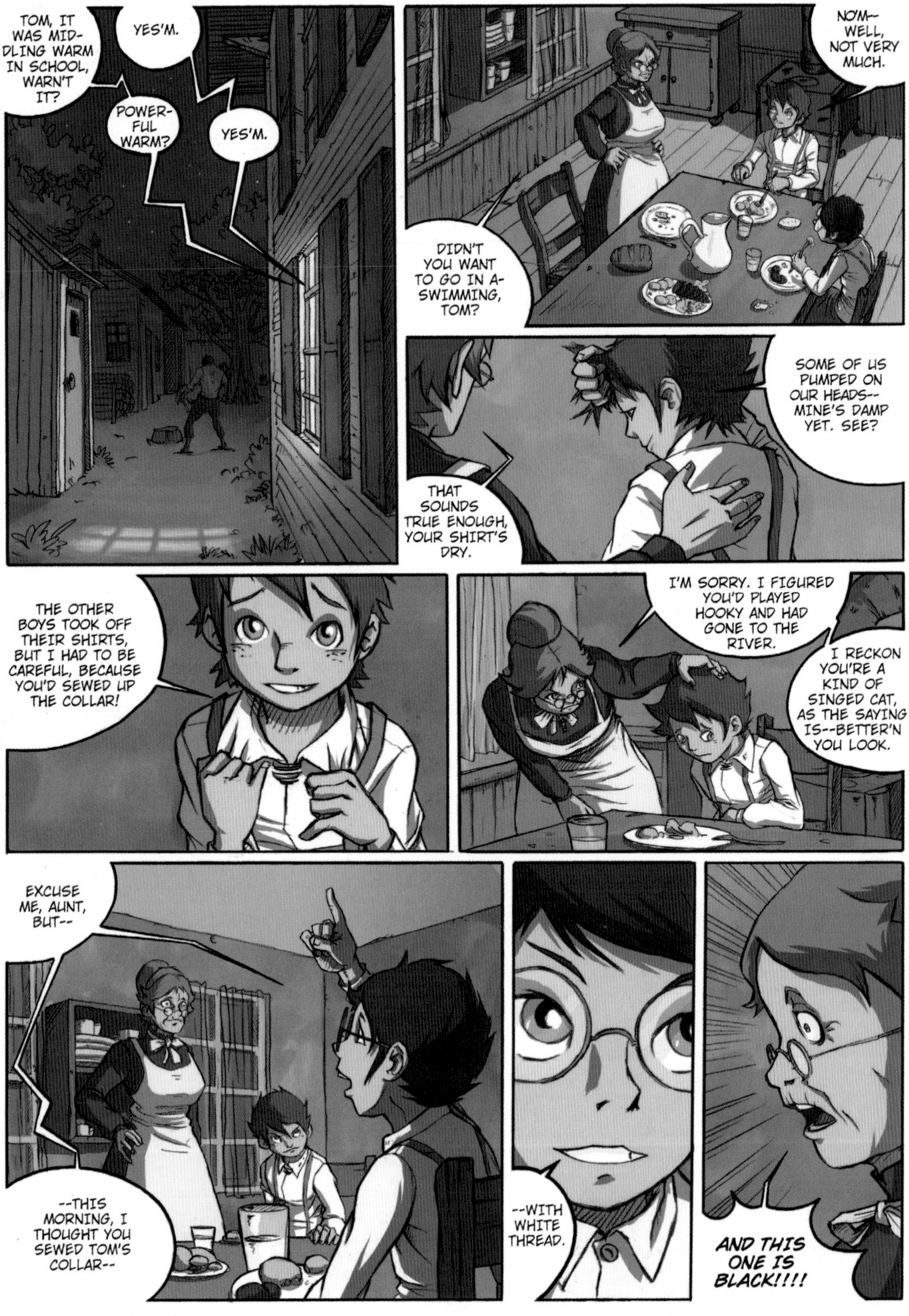
TOM, IT WAS MID-DLING WARM IN SCHOOL, WARN'T IT?
YES'M.
POWER-FUL WARM?
YES'M.
NO'M-- WELL, NOT VERY MUCH.
DIDN'T YOU WANT TO GO IN A-SWIMMING, TOM?
SOME OF US PUMPED ON OUR HEADS-- MINE'S DAMP YET. SEE?
THAT SOUNDS TRUE ENOUGH, YOUR SHIRT'S DRY.
THE OTHER BOYS TOOK OFF THEIR SHIRTS, BUT I HAD TO BE CAREFUL, BECAUSE YOU'D SEWED UP THE COLLAR!
I'M SORRY. I FIGURED YOU'D PLAYED HOOKY AND HAD GONE TO THE RIVER.
I RECKON YOU'RE A KIND OF SINGED CAT, AS THE SAYING IS--BETTER'N YOU LOOK.
EXCUSE ME, AUNT, BUT--
--THIS MORNING, I THOUGHT YOU SEWED TOM'S COLLAR--
--WITH WHITE THREAD.
AND THIS ONE IS BLACK!!!!

ROBERT LOUIS STEVENSON

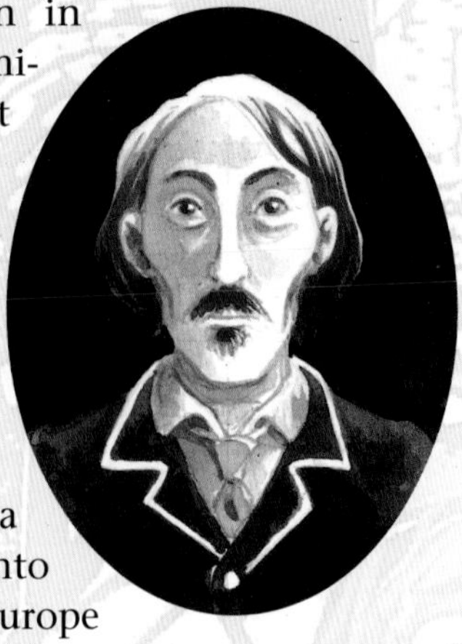

Robert Louis Stevenson was born in Edinburgh on November 13, 1859, to a family of upper-middle-class Calvinist Scots. At birth, Stevenson showed signs of pulmonary trouble, a condition which plagued him throughout his life. He briefly studied civil engineering, and was preparing for the bar when ill health interrupted his studies at Edinburgh University. He was never to return to the law; instead, Stevenson embarked upon a roving, bohemian existence which lasted into his thirties. Stevenson's travels through Europe during this time formed the basis of his first two books, *An Inland Voyage* (1879) and *Travels With a Donkey* (1879). In 1875, Stevenson settled into an artists' colony at Barbizon, France, and began writing for English magazines. In France, he met Fanny Van de Grift Osbourne, a married woman ten years his senior; Stevenson followed her in 1889 to San Francisco (a journey chronicled in *An Amateur Emigrant* in 1894). After Mrs. Osbourne obtained a divorce, they married and, in 1880, returned to Scotland. In rapid succession, Stevenson published several collections of essays and tales: *Virginibus Puerisque* (1881), *Familiar Studies of Men and Books* (1882), *New Arabian Nights* (1882), and *Silverado Squatters* (1883), his recollections of California. *Treasure Island* appeared in 1883; it was Stevenson's first successful and popular book, and established him as a prominent writer. 1885 saw the publication of *A Child's Garden of Verses* and *Dr. Jekyll and Mr. Hyde* (which sold 40,000 copies in six months); *Kidnapped* followed in 1886. Because of Stevenson's failing health, the couple decided in 1887 to return to America. During a brief stay, Stevenson wrote *The Master of Ballantrae* (1888), essays for Scribner's Magazine, and, with his stepson Lloyd Osborne, a farcical story, *The Wrong Box*. He and his wife then set out for the South Seas, finally arriving in Samoa in 1888. Except for a brief visit to Australia, Stevenson remained in Samoa during the last years of his life. He lived as a planter and chief of the natives, and was known as Tusitala, the Teller of Tales. In Samoa, Stevenson wrote *The Wrecker* (1892), again in collaboration with his stepson; *Island Nights Entertainments* (1893); and *Catriona* (1893), a sequel to *Kidnapped*. Stevenson was dictating *Weir of Hermiston* when he died of a cerebral hemorrhage on December 3, 1894. His *Letters* were published posthumously in 1895.

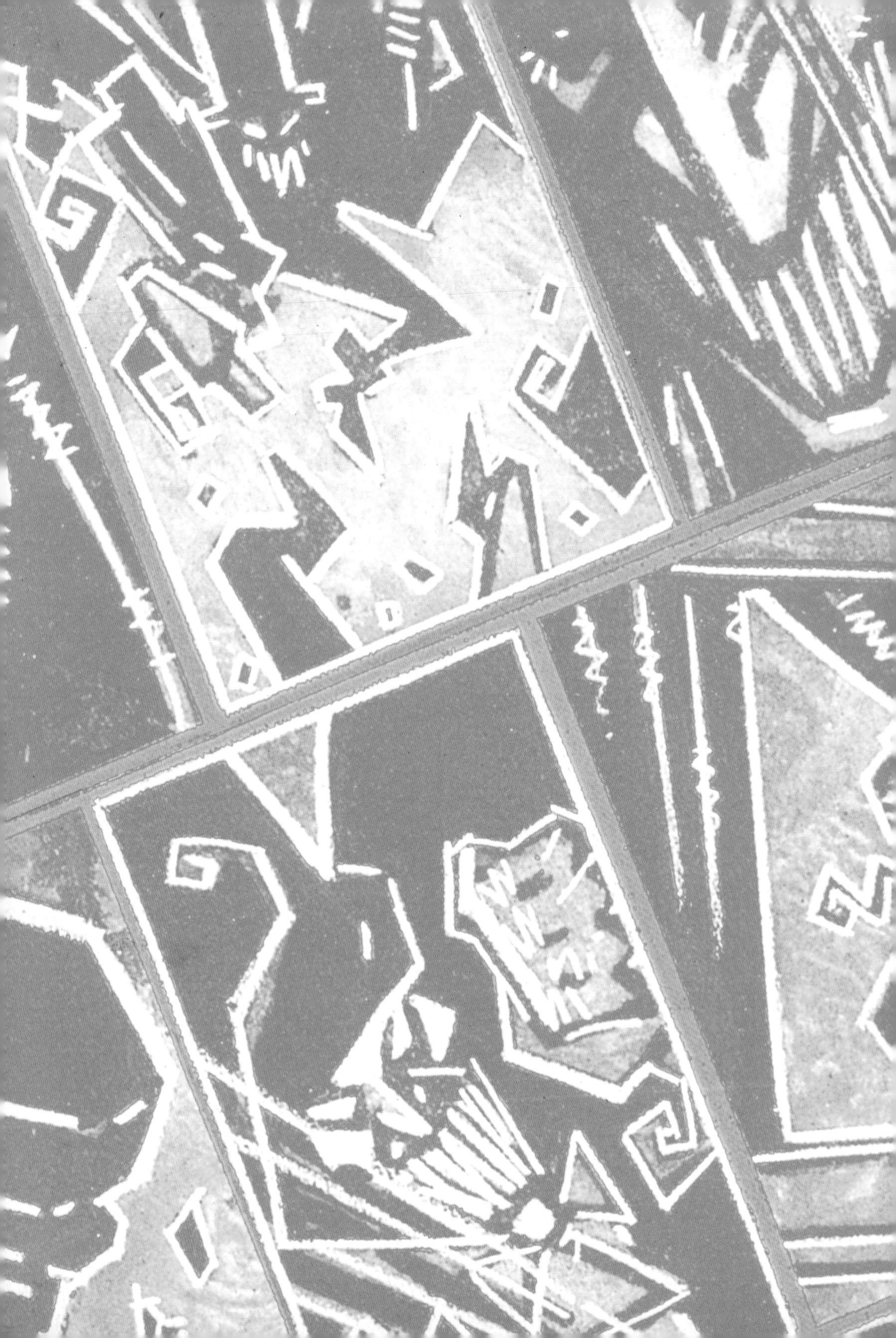